ONCE AGAIN AT THE Falls

USA TODAY BESTSELLING AUTHOR
BECKY MONSON

Other Books by Becky

Thirty-Two Going on Spinster
Thirty-Three Going on Girlfriend
Thirty-Four Going on Bride
Speak Now or Forever Hold Your Peace
Taking a Chance
Just a Name
Just a Girl
The Accidental Text
The Love Potion
How to Ruin the Holidays
Pumpkin Spice and Not So Nice

Connect with Becky

www.beckymonson.com

DEDICATION

To Rob.
My hubby, my best friend, my one and only.
I'm glad I found you when I did.

TIES THAT BIND

Friendship is a precious thing.
It's made and woven out of strings.
The kind of ties that can't be seen
But last in life through everything.
Made from the heart are strands of love,
A thread of kindness from above.
Knit together they create a bind,
Friendship that stands the test of time.
Because the world cannot see
This bond between you and me,
We'll take some string to weave together
In a band we'll wear forever.
Upon our wrists, these strings we'll place,
Giving our friendship a physical face.
A sign of friendship, strong and true,
These forever ties that bind me and you.

One

"YOUR FATHER AND I ARE getting a divorce."

This was my mother's greeting when I reluctantly answered the phone, and the third thing to add to my list of crappy things that had happened that day. The first on the list was walking out on my job—no notice, no nothing. But I had to. I *had* to. I couldn't have stayed there one more second and looked at Braydon's stupid, smug face.

The second crappy thing had been waiting for me in the mail, which I'd again waited too long to grab. I mean, it's almost always bills, and who wants to see those? Even worse than bills was the Christmas card and letter from my high school teacher, Miss Anna Cate. The news from my mentor was not good. The worst kind of news, actually.

And now my parents were getting divorced. I'd have been sure to write this all in my diary and mark it "worst day ever," if I even had a diary, which I didn't.

"Come again?" I asked, not sure I had heard my

1

mother correctly. Or maybe hoped I hadn't. I reached up and twisted some of my hair around my finger. A nervous habit, but I had a lot going on.

"I'm divorcing your father," she repeated, her tone firm. I could easily picture her face. The downturn of her lips, the creases between her brows.

"Are you sure?" I asked. It was kind of a dumb question, but in my defense, I wasn't thinking normally. The proverbial rug had already been nudging its way out from under my legs, and then my mom swooped in and dragged it full-force, leaving me to land right on my rear.

"London," she said, clearly irritated. "I'm quite sure."

"Um, okay," I said, unsure of what I could even say to that. I needed to hang up, to process this. I looked around my messy apartment, hoping for some way to get out of this conversation. But it offered nothing. No excuse to save me. So I plopped down on my bed, still wearing the Rachel Zoe black pant suit that I had put on that morning before work—back when life was still hopeful and bad things hadn't happened. Oh, to go back.

"Why are you getting divorced?" I asked, reaching up and pinching the bridge of my nose. I was feeling a headache coming on.

She sighed a big, hearty sigh. "It's been a long time coming. Your father and I . . . we will always love each other; we just can't tolerate each other anymore."

"You can't tolerate each other anymore?" I repeated, wondering briefly if maybe I was still sleeping and this was one of those stupid dreams you are so relieved to wake up from. My parents couldn't tolerate each other anymore? Are most marriages based on tolerance? What about love?

What about respect? When did toleration become the most important part of the equation? Maybe there was more to it and my mother didn't want to tell me.

"Oh my gosh, did Dad cheat on you?" I asked, my mouth speaking on its own accord—something that happened on a frequent basis for me.

"No! There's been no cheating. Not by either of us," she cut me off before I could ask if perhaps she had done the cheating. "Actually, there's been none of any of *that* for a long time. For either of us."

"Okay, Mom, ew," I said, swallowing hard. That was what every daughter in her mid-twenties wanted to hear about her parents.

"Oh, grow up, London," she said, incredulous. "Anyway, I'm calling because I need you to come home."

"Mom," I sighed, "I *am* coming home, remember?"

My plan had been to drive out to Phoenix on Christmas Eve, stay until two days after Christmas, and then drive back to San Francisco. I had taken a full week off from work, but I didn't think I could stomach being with my family for that long. Seeing my siblings would be hard with my older sister, Savannah, and her perfect children and husband, and my younger brother, Boston, whom I hadn't seen since he graduated top of his class from Stanford earlier that year. He already had a job in some fancy-shmancy brokerage firm in Scottsdale. Overachiever.

And then there was me. I was just London. Living by myself in a ridiculously overpriced closet (it wasn't big enough to call an apartment) and quitting a job yet again. This was job number five since graduating college. Of course, it wasn't like anyone in my family knew I'd quit my job earlier in the day. And it's not like I was going to say anything about it now because it would only add to the utter disappointment I had become. I was, by all definitions, failing at life.

"I know you're coming home for Christmas, but I need you to come home this weekend," my mom said with her no-nonsense tone.

"This weekend?" I asked, feeling panicked. The walls of my closet-sized apartment were suddenly feeling even smaller.

"Yes," she said, an unmistakable you'll-do-what-I-say tone to her voice.

"Why?" I asked.

"Because I need you. Everything is moving quickly. There's so much to do, so much stuff to separate. I need your help. Savannah can't, and I don't want to bother Boston."

Of course Savannah couldn't help. She never could. And my mother wouldn't even think of bothering her sweet baby Boston. Heaven forbid.

I, on the other hand, was an easy target. I had no strings attached—no children or significant other or new job to keep me busy. I had all the time in the world, according to my mother. And the truth was, I didn't have anything going on. No job to keep me busy, no boyfriend to speak of. Not since Braydon and I broke up. No way would I be able to stomach him being my new boss. That was a deal breaker. Not that Mom knew about any of that. I could tell her I had work to do on my Etsy shop, but since that hadn't made me any profit as of yet, and was more or less just a hobby, she'd never take that as an excuse.

But what was there to go home to? My parents were adults. They could work all this out between themselves. Why drag me into it, anyway? Honestly, a visit to the dentist sounded more pleasant than being engulfed in all this family drama. It was freaking Christmastime.

"Mom, I really don't think I can. I have, uh, work stuff," I lied, since that was really my only option.

"You can, and you must," she said.

And that was the way things were done with Melinda Walsh, contracts lawyer extraordinaire. Why couldn't she passive-aggressively guilt me into things like a normal mother? She was demanding, frustrating, and overzealous in her endeavors to rule over me. Well, maybe that was exaggerating a bit, but she had always been domineering, and I was kind of tired of it. Actually, I was *really* tired of it.

I looked down at the letter staring up at me from Miss Anna Cate. The other-other piece of bad news from this horrible day. My heart sank as I remembered her words. My mentor—my favorite teacher—was dying. She had one request—that I come back to Christmas Falls and sing the final song in the pageant at the community center. My initial thought was to tell her no. It wasn't that I didn't want to go back to Christmas Falls, I did. But I didn't know if I could handle seeing Miss Anna Cate in the state she was in. Dying. She had been one of the brighter—if not the brightest—spots of my early life. How could my heart take it?

But as Mommy Dearest was making her demands, I

had the sudden feeling that Christmas Falls might be the answer to all my problems. I could get away from San Francisco and the job I no longer had, away from my family and all the drama that would most definitely ensue, and go to the place—the only place—that had ever felt like home to me. Try as I might, in the eight years since I'd left, I could never find that feeling of belonging again.

Maybe I'd romanticized it. Maybe it wouldn't feel like home anymore. But there was only one way to find out.

"Well, actually, I wasn't going to tell you this because I didn't know how to break it to you," I gulped down my lie, "but I can't come home, Mom. I have to go to Christmas Falls."

"Christmas Falls?" she practically spat. "Why on earth would you want to go there?"

My mom was raised in the wealthy part of Denver, Colorado, and had always claimed to be a "city girl." She met my dad on a family vacation at a dude ranch near Gatlinburg where he worked in the summers. A small-town boy and a city girl. It was love at first sight, according to my dad. Apparently not so much anymore.

After years of doing the long-distance thing, they finally got married their sophomore year of college. After graduate school, they settled in Christmas Falls, unintentionally started a family not long after that, and it wasn't long before my mom wanted out of the small-town life. She said she found it stifling. After years of pestering, demanding, and ultimatums from my mom to my dad, we moved after my senior year and none of us had ever been back.

"I need to see Miss Anna Cate," I said.

"Miss Anna who?" she asked, disdain ringing through her tone.

"My music teacher? Throughout high school? My mentor from the community center?"

"Doesn't ring a bell."

And there it was. Miss Anna Cate meant the world to me back then. She was one of the most important people in my life. I can't say there had been a lot of people who had made such an impact on me, but Miss Anna Cate was definitely one who had. And my mother had no recollection. So typical.

"It doesn't matter. She needs me to come to Christmas Falls," I said. "She's dying, Mom. She wants to see me."

"Well, that's sad," my mother said, and to her credit, she did sound sincere. "Miss Anna Cate . . . Miss Anna Cate," she repeated her name as she tried to recall the woman that had meant so much to me.

"She had the shorter, graying hair? Led the choir? Ran the community center?" Short of sending her a picture, I wasn't sure anything would jog her memory.

"Oh yes," she said. "I remember now. She gave you that silly bracelet you wouldn't take off. I hated that thing."

Right. The bracelet. The one I didn't have anymore. Not that it mattered, it was years ago.

"Anyway, so you understand why I can't come home this weekend."

"Yes," she said, still lost in thought. "But you'll be home for Christmas." This was not said in the form of a question.

I closed my eyes tight, bracing myself. "Well . . . I'm not sure. She, uh, wants me to sing one last time in the pageant." My heart started racing, knowing this was going to go over about as well as a lead balloon.

"The pageant? That silly little show at the community center?"

"Yes, that one," I said, slightly annoyed. It was not a "silly little show." It was one of the highlights of Christmastime in Christmas Falls. The community center, Christmas spirit everywhere, singing my heart out with my best friend—well, my ex-best friend that I hadn't spoken to in years. I could never find a friendship like I had with Piper, not in the past eight years, even though I'd tried. Dear heavens, I'd tried.

"Wait . . . wasn't the pageant on Christmas Day?"

I cringed. I was kind of hoping she wouldn't put that together, and then I could text her about it later. I couldn't get yelled at via text. Well, I could, but it was less scary.

"Um, yes," I said rather timidly.

"London Jean Walsh, you will not be staying in Christmas Falls for Christmas. You will come home!" she demanded, her voice escalating with each word.

"I need to go to Christmas Falls," I said, a pleading tone to my voice.

"You need to come home!"

Oh yes, she was livid now. I briefly wondered if I should hang up. Maybe let her cool off.

That was the thing, though—Phoenix wasn't home. I never really lived there, only stayed there over summers and other school breaks. Northern California should have been my home since I had spent the last four years there, but that never felt right either. The only place I'd ever felt at home was Christmas Falls.

"Mom, this is kind of important," I said, holding the letter up as if she could see it. Miss Anna Cate needed me. How could I let her down? Even if I had just come up with the idea.

There was any easy fix for all of this—an easy way to get my mother down from her angry perch. I scrunched my face and said, "I'll take the first flight out the day after Christmas to Phoenix, okay? I'll even stay the whole week."

"The whole week?" I knew the second she said this that I was in the clear. I hadn't come home for an entire week in ages. I, on the other hand, was having a quick onset of heart palpitations. *An entire week?* Heaven help me.

"Yes, Mom, the whole week," I said, half-heartedly choking out the words. "I'll be there to do y'all's bidding."

She let out a huff. "Don't say 'y'all,'" she reprimanded. She never liked the fact that her children had gained Southern accents while living in Christmas Falls. Mine was almost gone at this point, but I did throw out a "y'all" every now and then. Mostly to annoy her.

"I've gotta go, Mom," I said, knowing we were heading down a petty road. First, it was correcting my grammar, next it would be telling me to stop chewing my nails, which, coincidentally, I was doing. "Tell Dad I love him . . . I mean, next time you see him."

I added the last part since I didn't know how all that

worked. It still hadn't set in—at twenty-six, my parents were not going to be together anymore. I felt some comfort in knowing I would be in Christmas Falls and could sort all of that out later. In my mind, and in reality.

"Well, okay," she said, sounding as if she still wasn't completely convinced. "Quick question, though—how are you getting so much time off work? I thought you could only take a few days?"

"What was that?"

"I said—"

"Sorry, mom, *shhhhhhh*! Bad *shhhhh* connection! We're going through a tunnel! *Shhhhhhhh.*"

"I thought you were at home?" she said, now yelling like people do when losing a phone connection. As if escalating your voice would even help.

I hung up quickly and powered off my phone, pretending the connection was lost. No way was I going to go explain all of that. Besides, she would never understand why I had quit. If they hadn't promoted Braydon, I'd probably still be sitting at my desk right now. It was a knee-jerk reaction, I know. I hadn't even given the guy a chance. But to have your ex-boyfriend as your boss? That was not a good idea. Not when things ended as poorly as they had. Actually, the bad idea was dating a coworker in the first place. But live and learn, right?

Not having a job lined up was probably not very wise either. Like I said, it was a spontaneous move. But I did have some money saved. At least there was that.

As I grabbed my laptop and pulled up the travel website I always used, I wondered, briefly, if I was making a mistake by not going to Phoenix. But my mind was made up. I was going to see Miss Anna Cate; I was going to sing in that Christmas pageant.

I was going home.

Two

I WAS HOME.

Thanks to the last-minute booking, I had to sit between a man who snored and a woman with a baby who cried intermittently throughout the entire red-eye flight. After, I picked up a rental car and drove the four hours from Nashville to Christmas Falls. If it hadn't been for energy drinks, I'm not sure I would have survived the drive.

As a kid, I'd always dreamed of staying in the bed and breakfast near Main Street. Poinsettia Cottage, owned by Randall and Betty Curtis, was one of the quaintest things I'd ever seen. The Curtises, long-time residents of Christmas Falls, lived in the two-story structure and rented out the remaining four bedrooms after their youngest daughter left for college. I was thrilled when they told me they had a room available, and even more thrilled to receive a discount for staying for more than one week.

Upon my arrival, Mrs. Curtis was fussing over some poinsettias in the front room. The cottage was decked from top to bottom in Christmas décor, and the house smelled of cinnamon and apples. It was cozy, warm and welcoming, and, in a word, heavenly. Nothing like the massive hotels in San Francisco. Even the quainter lodgings out there had nothing on this place.

"Welcome," Mrs. Curtis said when she saw me.

"Hi, Mrs. Curtis," I said, the thrill of being here raced through me.

She looked at me oddly, like she was trying to place me. Since I knew her name, she must have wondered if she knew me. I figured she wouldn't know me because I hadn't spent any time with her when I lived in Christmas Falls before. Her children were older than me—her youngest daughter was two years my senior—so there wasn't much of a reason for us to be acquainted. I knew of her only because I had always wanted to stay here. I explained as much to her after I introduced myself.

"Oh, well aren't we lucky to have you." She gave me a little wink. Her hair was mostly gray and short, and she wore one of those bright Christmas sweaters with reindeer on them and some of those polyester pants with the elastic waist that were all the rage among the older people in this town. There was something about comfort as you aged—like fashion, with all its constricting zippers and buttons and hem lines, just wasn't important anymore. I looked forward to that time, even though I currently loved everything about fashion.

Mrs. Curtis checked me in, handed me my key, and

gave me a quick tour of the cottage before taking me to my room and leaving me to get settled.

The room was beautiful. A large, four-poster bed took over most of the space, with a poinsettia bedspread covering it. On one side of the bed was a nightstand with a digital clock, and a dark green upholstered arm chair that looked worn and welcoming.

After putting my toiletries in the small but clean bathroom and unpacking my clothes into the dark armoire that was against the wall across from the bed, I decided I would venture out to the downtown area of Christmas Falls. I was so full of anticipation, my heart felt like it was going to burst. I was hopeful that the spirit of the season Christmas Falls was so well known for would still be there.

And hopefully I would see some familiar faces. Maybe I would even run into some people I knew – people that I used to work with, or some of my friends from high school. Maybe even Piper. If she was still here. Aside from Anna Cate, my biggest hope of returning to Christmas Falls was to see Piper.

But I didn't know if she lived here anymore. I'd never responded to Miss Anna Cate's letter before I left; I didn't have time to. My plan was to pay her a visit, maybe later today. Until I saw her, I had no idea if Piper would even be here, no idea if I would be singing a solo at the pageant . . . I may not have thought this through completely.

But now that I was here, I knew I'd made the right decision, pageant solo or not. Christmas Falls had not changed much. From the architecture and landscaping to the decor, it was like I'd stepped back in time. Almost as if time had frozen. The diner was still there, and so was Tinsel's coffee shop. The bookstore, the floral shop, the antique store—all here and all the same.

If anything, the Christmas spirit had grown even more in the quaint town. They now piped holiday music onto the street, and every square inch of the buildings on Main Street was covered with holiday lights. I couldn't wait to see it all at night. When I lived here before, Christmas Falls—or the Falls, as the locals sometimes called it—always had an air of the holidays no matter what time of year it was. But during the season, they went all out. That was definitely still the case.

The first familiar face I saw was Mr. Wilson, the feed store owner. His hair—crazy, white, and standing up all over his head—was unchanged from the last time I'd seen him eight years ago. He always did look like a mad scientist. My heart thrilled at the sight of him. He was still here, still doing the same thing in Christmas Falls. I waved at him, quite obnoxiously, and he squinted his eyes at me like he had no idea who I was. He always was a crotchety old thing; I didn't really expect him to remember me.

I continued my perusal of Main Street. Seeing the lit-up, carefully manicured potted bushes that dotted the street, and the care that was put into the exterior of the town, it felt so right to be here. Nothing like the streets of downtown San Francisco, with all the people just trying to get from one place to the next. There were no smiley greetings, no nods of acknowledgment. But here, everyone was smiling, minus Mr. Wilson, but that was always the case. It felt like home. And it felt like Christmas.

I couldn't remember a time since I left here when the holidays had felt this festive. It was never like this in Phoenix. Not with the palm trees, the sand, and the rock gardens. Not to mention the weather was always in the 60s. Sure, my parents decorated the house to the brim—giving even Clark Griswold a run for his money—even so, it never felt like Christmas there. Here in the Falls, I felt Christmas all around me.

My first stop was the bakery inside the grocery store, where I'd worked during the school year and on summer vacations while I was in high school. My favorite thing in the whole world, still to this day, was one of Mrs. Mitchem's sugar cookies. I had never had other cookies like them since leaving here, and I'd been to some famous bakeries in Northern California. But none of them held a candle to Mrs. Mitchem's. I hoped she was still here, still making all the baked goods for the town.

I walked toward the store with a hop in my step. I could feel adrenaline pulsing through me. I was in Christmas Falls where I belonged. I had made the right choice coming here, I could feel it in my bones.

The door to the quaint grocery store opened with a jingle—the same bells that had hung around the inside of the handle were still there. Their clinging and clanging filled me with melancholy, bringing back memories of working here and coming here with my friends.

And the smell! The smell of the yeasty bread and other baked goods wafted through the open door, and it was like I'd never left. I could almost see Piper coming through these doors and heading straight back to the bakery to hang out with me while I worked—back when things were right between us, before everything went wrong. I could picture Andy, my best guy friend at the time, trying to steal cookies when I wasn't looking. So many memories in this store. So many heartwarming, wonderful memories.

I walked to the back, up to the bakery counter, and dinged the bell that had been sitting on that counter since before I worked there. Around the corner, from where the pantry was, came Barbara Mitchem, she was still here, looking exactly the same. Her hair was up in the same perfectly coiffed bun; and she was wearing one of her signature aprons. This one had a ruffle around the bottom and purple and yellow butterflies dancing across the print. Her face was round and there may have been a few extra wrinkles, but her smile was just as welcoming as it always had been. I couldn't wait for her to see me. I couldn't wait for the reunion that was about to happen.

"Can I help you?" she asked as she approached me, the large bakery display case separating us.

"Hi!" I practically squealed. I sounded like a cross between a drowning pig and a duck.

"Hi," she said back, her face blank, no recognition in her eyes.

"It's me," I said, holding my hands out to present myself.

"Well, hello you," she said, giving me a wink.

"Mrs. Mitchem?" I asked, my head tilting slightly to the side, hoping to possibly jog her memory a bit. She had to remember me. I'd spent hours with this lady, every day.

While Miss Anna Cate was my mentor and favorite teacher, Mrs. Mitchem had been like a second mom to me.

"Can I help you?" she asked again. I blinked. She blinked back.

Disappointment swirled in my belly. I had pictured a very different scenario than what was happening. I'd figure there would be some hugging, probably a dash of joyous laughter (it was the holidays, after all), and maybe even a few tears in my mind's-eye version of how this was supposed to go down. Instead, there were a few awkward head bobs, an ever-growing awkward smile from Mrs. Mitchem, and me standing there not knowing what to say.

"Oh, I remember!" Mrs. Mitchem said, her eyes now sparkling with recognition. She remembered me! "You're here for the cake!"

"I—"

"Hold on a second, I have it in the walk-in." And with that, she about-faced and walked back to the large walk-in cooler.

"Mrs. Mitchem, I—"

"Hold on dear, I can't hear you back here," she said loudly. I could see the top of her bun bobbing up and down behind the large baking racks as she walked into the cooler.

It wasn't long before she came back with a half-sheet sized cake box and promptly placed it into my arms—which apparently looked to be awaiting the cake, when in reality I was just standing there dumbfounded.

"I, uh," I stammered as I looked down at the cake. The base frosting was white, and the whimsical swirling border was done in red. In the center, a Christmas tree had been hand drawn with icing, and round balls serving as ornaments were in bright colors of red, green, and yellow. To fill in the other space, there were red poinsettia flowers and small white gardenias, all made out of frosting. The words "Merry Christmas" were written in perfect cursive to the left of the tree.

I stared at it and my mouth literally watered. Mrs. Mitchem made the best sugar cookies I had ever had, and her cakes came in second, in my book.

I looked back up at her, the cake still in hand.

"Is something wrong?" she asked, probably due to the look of utter confusion on my face mixed with a little drool.

"This isn't my cake," I said, handing the cake back to her.

"Oh no, oh dear," she fussed. "Did I make the wrong cake again?" She took the cake from me, her eyebrows knitted together with concern.

"No, it's not that, the cake is beautiful. I just never ordered a cake."

"Oh," she said, placing the cake on the top of the display counter. "Well, then, what can I help you with?" she asked me once again.

I let out a breath. This was so not going like I had envisioned. "Mrs. Mitchem, it's me," I said, pointing to myself. "London Walsh."

"London Walsh?" she asked, a look of shock on her face as she looked my face over, even leaning in to get a better view. "My London Walsh?" she asked, now pointing to herself.

"Yes," I said, delighted. "It's me, Mrs. Mitchem."

She just stared at me. "But my London Walsh had black hair." She eyed me, as if trying to find the missing pieces to a puzzle.

"Well, yes, my hair is a little lighter," I said, reaching up and twirling my finger through my golden-brown hair with the caramel blonde highlights.

"And your makeup," she said, still taking in my face.

"Yeah, I stopped doing all that black eyeliner and smoky look a long time ago," I said. My brown eyes were now highlighted by neutral colored eyeshadow and mascara. Also gone was the fake nose ring (my mom wouldn't let me get a real one), and the black fingernail polish.

"And . . . and your clothes?" She gestured with her hand at my outfit.

Yes, gone were the ripped up black jeans, the dark colored tee-shirts, and the Converse I'd worn nearly every day of high school. I'd gotten rid of that stuff a long time ago. I was currently wearing something a lot more girly—light colored skinny jeans, a white pea-coat covering a long violet tunic sweater, and high-heeled, knee-high brown leather boots.

She looked me over again, coming back to my eyes as she took me in. As if with magic, her scrunched up face of confusion morphed into one of pure delight. She recognized me.

"Well, oh my goodness, London Walsh! My London," she said, finally seeing me. She reached for me and pulled me into a huge hug, rocking me back and forth as we both laughed. When we stepped away, I could have sworn she wiped a tear from the corner of her eye.

Now that was more like it.

"Tell me how you're doing. Tell me everything! What have you been up to these past . . ." she cut herself off as she appeared to be doing some calculating in her mind.

"Eight years," I said, helping her add up the years.

"Eight years . . . my goodness. That's a long time. Why haven't you come back to see me before now?"

I shook my head. "You know, I always wanted to come back, I could just never make it with my family in Phoenix and my job in San Francisco." The truth was I never even tried. I should have tried harder.

"You work in San Francisco?" she asked, her eyes wide with excitement. She ushered me to the back of the kitchen, where she was currently frosting another cake, so we could catch up.

I filled her in on the past eight years of my life. Leaving out some of my bigger failings—never feeling settled, going through five different jobs, my parents' impending divorce. I knew I could tell her all of these things, but at the moment I wanted her to be proud of me, even if there wasn't much to be proud of.

"Are you still takin' those picture thingies?" she asked.

"Yes," I nodded. "Still taking the picture thingies."

Back in high school I'd started taking pictures of pretty things, like flowers, butterflies, or beautiful landscapes, and then I'd put them in Photoshop and "goth them all up" as my mom used to say. I'd change the colors to deep hues of purple, black, and blue, and added overlays that were dark and gave them an air of mystery. I suppose it was a little . . . goth. They were my teenage expression of how I felt about the world, or so I would tell people. Really, I just liked the art part of it all. To take something bright and cheerful and turn it into something that was moody and brooding but still beautiful in its own way, had been a great outlet for me. And it still was. So much so that I sold prints on Etsy, although I'd yet to really turn a profit. So far, I'd just made a sale here and there to cover costs.

"So, what brings you back to the Falls?" she asked.

"Miss Anna Cate," I said, and by the look of her crestfallen eyes, I knew right away she was well aware of the situation. I'm sure everyone knew—word got around in this small town.

"And how is Piper?" she asked, clearly wanting to change the subject. "I haven't seen her in ages – although I've seen her folks around town,"

I smiled, probably sheepishly. "You know, I don't really know."

"What?" She tsked at a blob of icing that she dropped on the cake she was decorating and probably at the truth bomb I'd just blasted. "But you were thick as thieves, the best of friends. What happened?"

"I haven't seen or heard from Piper in eight years," I said. And even though it had been so long, a pang of sadness ran through me, settling in my lower belly. I had a lot of regrets in my life, but losing her friendship was one of the biggest.

"Well now, that's just sad," said Mrs. Mitchem. She'd grabbed a small flat knife and scooped her frosting mistake right off the cake and replaced it with a perfectly piped round ball. If only I could wipe away past mistakes as easily as that.

We chatted more and she even let me decorate a few sugar cookies, just like old times. I still remembered how to frost them the way she liked. Not like I could forget. I had probably frosted thousands of them during my time in this kitchen.

"Don't be a stranger," she said as she handed me a brown box full of sugar cookies. I planned to take them back to my room at the cottage and eat until I was sick.

I walked out of the grocery store feeling happy, warm, and wonderful all around. My reunion with Mrs. Mitchem may not have started out like I'd envisioned, but it ended even better than I could have hoped.

Three

I SPENT THE REST OF the evening walking around town, running into plenty of folks I identified immediately. Not one single person recognized me in return. Not Georgie from the floral shop. Not the permanent Christmas Falls fixture, retired teacher Ida Brown, who actually yelled, "WHO THE HECK ARE YOU?" when I waved at her. Not the Schnuks, who still owned the antique store. I thought for sure they'd recognize me, but nope. No one did. It was, by all accounts, super depressing.

I wanted so badly to come back to Christmas Falls and have it be just like old times. To feel like I did when I lived here before. To feel like home. Instead, I'd spent most of my time thus far trying to get people to remember me. I even pulled up a picture of me from high school that I had my mom text me. Everyone remembered that girl— the angsty, over-dramatic, goth girl I used to be—but it was hard for them to reconcile that with the woman

24

standing in front of them. It was disheartening and frustrating, and it made me second guess my decision to come out here.

Maybe I should have done more social media stuff—connected with more people. Then this change of mine wouldn't have been such a shock. But I didn't get into that stuff much because I didn't have anything good to post about myself, and I didn't want to watch a bunch of people living the life I wanted to live. Whatever that was.

It was after eating my third sugar cookie, while lying on the comfortable bed in my room, that I decided I would go see Miss Anna Cate tomorrow instead of today. I'd give her a big hug and tell her that due to some unforeseen circumstances, I needed to go back to San Francisco and wouldn't be able to do the pageant after all. I'd get to see her one last time, let her know how much she meant to me, and she'd hopefully understand that I needed to go.

It was painfully clear Christmas Falls was no longer home and was now a town where I was unknown. All of the heart-warming feelings and pictures in my head of how things would go down once I got here were not coming to pass.

I should have stayed home and helped my mom like she'd wanted me to. Although the thought of doing that made me feel even more crappy.

My mouth was feeling sugar coated after the three cookies I had downed, and I needed to brush my teeth. Imagine my annoyance level when the contents of my toiletry bag failed to include my toothbrush. There was another thing to add to what was becoming a long list of why this trip was sucking. Big time.

I went downstairs to the front room to ask if they had an extra one. There I found Mrs. Curtis dusting one of the tiny Christmas villages she had set up in the front window of the cottage. Of course, I must have temporarily forgotten this was Christmas Falls, and no place here would have the kind of complimentary items other large chain hotels would. She told me she could send Randall, who was yet to be seen, but I told her I could go grab one from the grocery store.

I'd already put on my pajamas, having completely given up on the day, so I pulled my white wool peacoat on over my PJs, slipped on my Uggs, and off I went. I decided while I was there I should probably stock up on some essentials, like water and some snacks for my room. I wasn't sure when I was going to find a flight back, and I figured I probably had at least a couple more days in this town.

While inspecting the snack aisle, looking for some chocolate covered almonds (because I'd already eaten the sugar cookies, might as well top it off with some chocolate), I ran smack dab into someone. A *he* someone, to be more precise.

"So sorry," I said, looking toward the ground as I realized I had knocked a bag of chocolate covered almonds out of his hand. "Where did you find these?" I asked the stranger I'd just plowed into as I bent over and picked up the bag, handing it back to the man.

I nearly dropped it again when I saw who the owner of the almonds was. "Andy?"

The lanky boy I once knew now had broad shoulders framing his tall figure. I did a double take, wondering if I was mistaken, but it was definitely him. His same hazel eyes and dark brown hair, the same pair of square-rimmed glasses he always wore perched on his nose. This was Andy Broll, for sure.

He looked at me, and I braced myself for the who-the-heck-are-you response I was surely about to get.

"London?" he asked, pulling his brows together. "London Walsh?"

"Yes," I said, feeling a sudden desire to jump up and down and squeal like a sorority sister. "You recognize me?"

"Yeah . . . yes, of course," he said. A full smile took over his face as his eyes moved over me, taking me all in.

"How are you here?" he asked.

"I took a plane," I said, a teasing grin on my face.

"Come here," he said, opening his arms wide to give me a hug, and I *so* needed a hug right then. I basically threw myself into his arms.

It wasn't graceful in the slightest, but it was exactly what I needed. The hug was tight, warm, and genuine. Andy felt strong and manly. There was some definite muscle action happening there. This was nothing like the skinny kid I used to hang out with.

"I'm so happy you recognized me," I said as we let go of each other.

"Why wouldn't I recognize you?" he asked, a confused look on his face.

"No one else has so far," I said, adding a super pathetic shrug for emphasis.

"Well, I mean, your hair is different," he said

reaching up and gently touching a lock of my brown-highlighted hair.

"Yeah, I got rid of the black," I said, feeling utterly thrilled to have someone recognize me—and Andy, of all people.

"And the makeup," he made a circle around his face with his index finger.

"Got rid of all that too," I said.

"I like," he said, using the words I used to say to him in high school. I beamed. "But you're still you," he said. "I still see London."

He smiled brightly again, and oh, how I'd missed that smile. At that moment, I couldn't believe I had ever lost touch with him. I couldn't even remember how it had happened.

"Why are you—"

"How are—"

We started at the same time and then both chuckled.

"You go first," he said.

"How are you?" I said, tucking hair behind my ear, feeling suddenly self-conscious of the fact that I was standing in the grocery store in my pajamas. In my defense, I hadn't thought I'd run into anyone I knew, and even if I had, I figured the chances of them recognizing me were pretty much zilch.

"I'm good," he said, head bobbing up and down.

"Are you here seeing your family?" I asked, wondering if the Brolls still lived in the same house—the one next door to the house I grew up in.

"Yeah, well . . . yes, I'm here to see them, but I actually moved back last week."

"Really? From where?"

"I was in Chicago. I took a job at Blackstock Resort—the big place up in Gatlinburg. I . . . uh . . . work with Piper, actually." He reached up and rubbed the back of his neck, obviously wondering if bringing up her name was the best idea.

But hearing her name come out of his mouth sent a jolt through me. "Piper? She's in town?"

"Yeah, she's back. Got a kid and everything." He rocked back and forth on his heels.

"Piper has a child?" I couldn't believe what I was hearing.

"A son," he said.

"She's married?"

"Divorced, from what I've gathered."

Piper was divorced? How had that happened?

"Have you heard about anyone else from school?" I had no idea what any of my old friends were up to. How sad it had come to that.

"Nah," he said. "I haven't heard anything."

Typical male. Although Andy hadn't hung out with all of us much. He had his group of friends, and I had mine. And when we weren't with them, we were with each other.

"How are you, though? What brings you here?" he asked, gesturing at the grocery store we were in. I looked over at the checkout counter to see a teenager I didn't know giving us a dirty look. Must have been close to closing time.

"I think the store is closing," I said, pointing to the front and the teenager with the death stare on his face.

"Right," he said, holding up a loaf of bread. "My mom needed some bread for tomorrow."

"You're living at home?" I asked, not meaning to sound as accusatory as it had come out.

"Yeah," he said, "temporarily, of course."

"That must be weird," I said, picturing myself living with my parents and feeling sick to my stomach at the thought.

"It totally is. My room is exactly the same," he said. "Creepy, right?"

"Totally creepy," I said with a laugh.

We made our way to the front of the store and he checked out while I ran to grab a toothbrush. I had completely forgotten what I had come here for. The death-stare teenager was not thrilled.

We checked out and made our way outside, the grumpy teen locking the door as we left and switching the open sign to closed. We stood in front of the store, grocery bags dangling from our wrists, the wintry night air moving around us.

"So, what brings you to the Falls?" Andy asked.

"I came to see Miss Anna Cate."

"Oh yeah," he nodded, a sad look on his face. "My mom told me about that."

"It's so sad," I said.

"Which way are you walking?" he asked as he noticed that I was starting to dance around in my boots a bit, trying to keep warm.

"I'm staying at Poinsettia Cottage." I gestured with my head in the direction of the home, knowing Andy knew exactly where it was.

"Ah yes, the Poinsettia Cottage."

"Well, there was so much to pick from," I said, my voice oozing sarcasm. There was an inn, but one time, back in high school, they were shut down for a cockroach infestation, and I could never get that out of my head, even after they were able to get rid of them. So there was no way I was staying there.

He smiled and it was the same old Andy smile—the one I remembered from when we were younger. But it now fit better in proportion to his face. It was less toothy and yet still incredibly endearing.

"Do you—" he started and then cut himself off.

"What?" I asked, feeling slightly breathless as I tried to keep myself warm. I should have worn a hat. I had the cutest one that went with my peacoat.

"Do you want to go to the diner?"

"Yes," I said, a little too agreeably. But this was Andy, and I didn't need to play it cool with him.

"Lead the way," he said, gesturing in the direction of the diner.

31

Four

I CAN'T REMEMBER THE FIRST time I met Andy. My family moved into the house next door to the Brolls when I was six, so it was probably around then. Although we were in the same grade, we were in different classes. That set the tempo for our friendship. At school, we barely saw each other. At home, we were nearly inseparable. I can still remember what six-year-old Andy looked like back then—a skinny little kid who wore black-rimmed, square-framed glasses, much like the ones he had on now. His dark curly hair was a little unrulier back then and his hazel eyes and toothy grin were a bit out of proportion for his face.

We did the normal kid stuff, building forts in our backyards, riding our bikes into town, making up stupid games we'd purposely not teach to my brother Boston or Andy's younger brother, Nick, which would make them both so mad. It was us against them.

We loved riding our bikes into town. There, we'd go to the falls – the namesake for our town – and swim in the river and play in the pool that the waterfall spilled into. We would catch tadpoles in the summer and trap spring lizards. Only when I was older did I realize those lizards were actually salamanders.

One time, one of the traps we set up accidentally killed one of the lizards, and it made me sad, but Andy . . . he was devastated. He made us dig a hole next to the falls and give it a proper burial. He made me sing "Amazing Grace" (which I only knew the first few words for, so I just repeated it), and he gave a little sermon. That was Andy, though. He could make me laugh like no other person, but he also had the softest side to him. The side that cared about the life of one single spring lizard when there were hundreds around.

I had always been more of a tomboy back then, so we got along famously. As we got older, I got into more girly stuff when I started spending time with Piper and some of the other girls from school, but the dynamic I had with Andy stayed the same. With Andy, I didn't have to get into all that drama girls so often do. Our friendship was easy. It was never a brother/sister-like friendship because we never fought or took each other for granted. It was just simple.

"Well, what do we have here," Clara said as she saw Andy and me enter the diner, the same old bell chiming as the door swung shut behind us. I was thrilled to see that she was still here. The diner just wouldn't have been the same without sassy Clara. She had been working at the only restaurant on Main since before I moved here. "If it isn't Andy Broll," she reached up and pinched his cheek. "Didn't you just turn out handsome?"

Her curly graying hair bounced around her shoulders as she talked to us, her tacky sweater matching the equally tacky Christmas decor that was way overdone for the space. In the background, soft country Christmas tunes played on the jukebox. It was all still the same, and I loved it.

"I go by Andrew now," Andy said, shaking the hand Clara held out for him. That made my gaze dart up to his, and he looked at me almost as if he wanted to see my reaction to that.

"It's good to see you, Clara," he said as we walked to the booth where she told us to sit. "You remember London?" he asked, gesturing to me.

She looked me up and down, no signs of recognition on her face.

"Come on," Andy said, pointing to me. "It's London Walsh—we were always in here together," he gestured toward the counter where we used to sit.

"Sorry, darlin'," she said, a kind smile on her face. "I do recognize the name, though."

"No worries," I said. "It was a long time ago, anyway."

"I do pride myself on not forgetting a face," she said. "Not sure why I can't seem to recall yours."

"Well, the obvious answer is your memory isn't what it used to be," Andy said, adding in a flirty smile so she'd think the jab was a joke. But I knew better. That was always his trick. And it worked; she slapped him on the arm playfully.

"Well, it's good to see you both in here," she said. "What can I get ya?"

We placed our order, which was the same order from high school. A chocolate shake for me, vanilla for him, and a basket of fries to share with the diner's homemade ranch dressing for dipping.

It went well with my current diet of sugar cookies and aided in helping me eat my feelings.

I looked around the diner, searching for anything that might have changed. Except for a new coat of paint, it had the same ambiance it always did. It was like stepping back in time. Back in the day, we came here all the time, Andy and I. Frequently Piper would join us, and she'd order the hot chocolate or steal some of my shake.

"See?" I said as Clara walked away. "No one recognizes me." I let out a big dramatic breath.

"I've gotta say, I didn't really believe you, but now I've seen it with my own eyes," Andy said.

"And she recognized you right away," I said pointing randomly behind me in the vicinity of Clara. "Although you've probably been in here more than I have in the past eight years."

"Nope, it's my first time back since high school."

"Liar."

"Well, maybe once or twice," he said, that teasing grin on his face.

I huffed. "Well anyway, I'm sure they recognize you because you've worn the same glasses since I can remember. Of course people are going to remember those," I say, gesturing toward his square-rimmed, black glasses.

"I think they remember me for my smile and my charm," he said, a note of flirtation in his tone.

"Oh yeah, that's totally it," I deadpanned. "I'm pretty sure it's the glasses."

"Pretty sure?"

"Like one hundred percent sure."

"Ouch," he said, and then he reached up and dramatically pushed his glasses up his nose, very librarian like. I smiled brightly and he gave me a smile back. Maybe it *was* his smile people remembered . . . I could never forget it, that was for sure.

"And what's the deal with 'I go by Andrew now,'" I said, doing a terrible job of imitating him.

"It just sounds more professional," he said.

"Well, I'm calling you Andy."

"Fine by me."

"Good, because Andrew doesn't suit you. It sounds too grown up."

"Well I am, in fact, a grownup," he said.

"Says who?" I quipped and he grinned in return. It was just like old times—we had gone right back to the same banter, the same energy between us. I had missed this.

"So, London Walsh. Back in Christmas Falls," Andy said, placing his chin atop his fists, elbows on the table, his hazel eyes looking inquisitively at me.

"Yep. I'm back," I said, copying his posture.

"And what do you think?"

"It really hasn't changed."

"Right?"

"I mean, there are a few things. But really, it's like

stepping back in time," I said. Andy nodded his head in agreement.

"How's your family?" he asked.

"They're pretty good. Well, I mean ... my parents are getting divorced."

"What? Really?" His eyes were wide behind his glasses.

"Yep," I said. "They couldn't *tolerate* each other anymore, apparently."

"When did you find this out?" he asked.

"Um . . . yesterday?" I pulled my eyebrows in and down. Was it only yesterday that I talked to my mom and made the rash decision to come here? It seemed like at least a week ago.

"Yesterday?"

"Yeah. Crazy, right? I mean, I'm twenty-six and my parents are getting divorced." I still hadn't let that all sink in. I think I was in the denial phase.

"Wow, I don't think I could have predicted that one. I mean, your parents always seemed happy when they were here," Andy said.

I shrugged one shoulder. "They probably were. A lot can change in eight years."

"True," he agreed. "What about Savannah? Boston?" Andy was really the only friend of mine who knew much about my siblings, having been right next door. Except for Piper, of course. She'd spent a lot of time at my house— enough time for my siblings to annoy us thoroughly—and they fulfilled their sibling-duties well. Luckily, I never had to endure middle school and high school with either of them as Savannah was four years older than me and Boston was four years younger.

"Sav's living near my parents in Arizona. She's married, has two kids—Rome and Phoenix." I pulled up one side of my mouth in a half grin, wondering if he remembered.

Andy's mouth fell open. He remembered. "She didn't."

"Yep. She sure did." I drew out the last part for emphasis, adding my best Southern twang as I did.

My siblings and I were all named after the cities we were conceived in, which my parents thought made for a good story. I found it to be a super gross story. I mean, that's not something people need to know. I'd thought Savannah felt the same way, but apparently not. At least Rome was kind of cool for a boy. A cool place to be conceived as well. But poor Phoenix . . . she had to live in the town she was conceived in and then named after.

Andy chuckled, shaking his head while he did. "And Boston?"

"Boston graduated from college in June and started a job in Scottsdale. I think he's into bond trading, or something way over my head."

"And what about you?" He took his elbows off the table and leaned back in the booth. "Fill me in on what I'm sure is London's very exciting life," he said, the last part sounding like a sports announcer.

I laughed and relaxed back in the booth as well. "Um, not exciting . . . no."

"Really? Why not?"

I looked down at the table, my eyes focusing on the

laminate covering with its Christmas tree pattern. It was in dire need of refurbishing.

I looked back up at Andy. "It's not bad, just not exciting."

He pondered for a second, his eyes steady on me. "Where are you living?"

"I'm in San Francisco, actually."

"So not in Arizona?"

"That was by design," I said. And that was true, I didn't want to be near Phoenix, front and center for all the family drama. Although my mother called me constantly to make sure I was abreast of any and all situations. Near or far, there was no getting away from it in the Walsh family.

"Where are you working these days?"

I gave him a sheepish grin. "I'm . . . between jobs."

"Oh." He lifted an eyebrow. "Where were you working before?"

I let out a breath. Might as well talk about it, even though I'd rather not. "I was working as the growth marketing manager for a small software startup." I purposefully left out that this had been my fifth job since college graduation.

"What happened?"

"I quit."

"Why?"

I let out a slow breath. "My ex-boyfriend was promoted to be my boss."

"Oh," he said, nodding his understanding.

"Yeah," I agreed.

"And when was that?"

"Um . . . yesterday."

"So yesterday you quit your job, found out that your parents are getting divorced—"

"And finally opened the letter from Miss Anna Cate telling me all about how she's doing," I interjected.

"Wow, that's quite the day," he said. "You deserve an award or something. Clara!" he called, waving over at Clara, who was behind the counter talking to a man I didn't recognize sitting on one of the stools. "Give this girl extra whipped cream on her shake, please. On me," he said with a wink. Clara didn't even acknowledge him.

"What about you?" I asked wanting to steer the conversation away from me. "Still burying spring lizards?"

The corners of his mouth turned up, and then he chuckled. "You remembered that."

"Of course I do. I think of it every time I see a lizard."

"Are there many in San Fran?"

"Sadly, no."

"Well, since there's no money to be made in lizard burial, I got into computers," he said.

It turns out, as I was informed, that my little Andy—who was not so little anymore—graduated from college with a degree in information systems. He moved to Chicago after that, where he worked for a start-up tech company that eventually became quite the heavy hitter for customer relationship management software. He made a nice sum when the company went public three years ago. His life, at least on paper, seemed like it was right on track. The map of my life looked like one of those loopty-loop roller coaster rides.

"So, what made you come back here from Chicago?"

I asked, wondering why he would ever leave a place he talked so fondly of.

"I never felt like Chicago was home, you know?" he said.

I did know. I knew all too well.

"No friends? No . . . girlfriend?" I don't know why it was hard for me to ask that. It wasn't like Andy and I had never dated people when we were in high school. It just felt weird to ask him now that we were adults.

"Yes to the friends, no to the girlfriend. Not by the time I left there," he said. "I had great friends, but the city life . . . it just wasn't for me."

I'd never really thought of it, but maybe the big city life wasn't for me either. Maybe that was my problem. Big cities always seemed like where I wanted to be. I remember visiting Nashville with my mom back when we lived in Christmas Falls. All the big buildings and the energy of the people walking around—it felt magical. It probably didn't help that my mom kept telling me about how much she missed the city life when we'd go for a visit. Living in a big city, though, that was a whole different experience. I loved it at first, but lately it had become almost too much. Too many people, too many buildings, too many cars.

"And now you're back," I said to Andy.

"I'm back," he said, spreading his lean but muscular arms out. "And I'm working at the resort, doing their IT."

Clara interrupted us when she set down our shakes and fries. She brought me a small bowl filled to the brim with more whipped cream and told Andy it was on the house. I'd forgotten that nothing ever got by that woman.

We chatted as we ate the fries and enjoyed the shakes. It felt so good to be here with Andy. It was just like old times, the same banter, the same jokes. I had friends in San Francisco. But I never connected with them like I had with Andy, or Piper. The friendships I made all those years ago were some of the best I'd ever had. They should have withstood the test of time, yet somehow they hadn't. It made me sad to think that we'd lost touch. And that I hadn't even tried.

After closing down the diner, with Clara giving us a death stare similar to the teenager at the grocery store, Andy walked me back to the cottage, claiming that it wasn't safe for me to walk by myself. I doubted there had been a crime committed in Christmas Falls since its founding. But I let him walk me, because it did feel safe, and also because I found myself not wanting the night to end. If anything, this night alone had made the trip worth it.

"How long are you in town?" Andy asked when we stopped in front of the cottage and I fished around in my purse for my room key. The house was mostly dark except for a lone light that could be seen from the window, probably there so guests could find their way around the place after the Curtises went to bed.

"Well," I said, drawing out the word. "Miss Anna Cate asked me to sing in the pageant."

"So you'll be here for Christmas?" he asked, his eyebrows raised in surprise.

"That was the original plan, but . . ." I trailed off.

"But what?"

"I was thinking of visiting Miss Anna Cate tomorrow and then just taking off."

"And not sing in the pageant?"

"I don't know," I said. "This trip has been a bust so far . . . until I ran into you," I gestured at him with my hand. "And I just . . . I don't know." I looked down at the room key now in my palm. The street light reflected off its metal exterior.

"You have to sing in the pageant. You need to where the Santa hat and sing Silent Night. At the very least, you need to stay for that."

"That's like at the bottom of the list of reasons for staying," I said.

"Stay," he said. "I mean, I just found you." He reached a hand up and briefly touched my arm, his fingers gliding softly over my coat. "And you could have Christmas with my family."

The realization that I had no real plans for Christmas dawned on me just then. What *was* I going to do on Christmas day? Was I just going to spend it alone? By myself at the Poinsettia Cottage? I supposed I could have spent it with Miss Anna Cate, but as far as she knew I wasn't even in town. This trip really had not been thought through.

"Thanks for the offer," I said. "I don't want to intrude."

"Not an intrusion, my mom and dad would love to see you. And Nicky too," he said. "At least think about it. You came all this way. You might as well see it through to the end. And you have me to hang out with now."

"I don't know . . ."

"Come on. Stay. I'll make it worth it if you do."

"I'll think about it," I said, giving him a grin.

We exchanged numbers and he told me he'd be calling me tomorrow. Before he left, he leaned in and gave me a kiss on the cheek, something he had never done before. But maybe this is what adult Andy and London did. I reached up on my tiptoes afterward and returned the kiss on his cheek, which I didn't think anyone did in any culture, but it was too late, the deed was done.

Five

I STAYED UP LATE THAT night binge watching a *Friends* marathon and slept in until noon the next day because I had nothing better to do. Then I hung out in my room for a few more hours, not sure I wanted to venture out into town and have no one recognize me again.

I popped downstairs to say hello to the Curtises and secretly hoped that they had some breakfast leftover because I was starving. I found Mr. Curtis restringing some lights that apparently had died, and Mrs. Curtis was making gingerbread cookies in the kitchen.

"It smells great in here," I said as I entered the kitchen area. The kitchen wasn't grand or fancy, but it was just the right size for a bed and breakfast. There was a swinging door next to the refrigerator that led to a small dining area with three small four-top tables that barely fit the space.

"Well thank you, London," Mrs. Curtis beamed at

me. "Would you like something to eat? You never came down for breakfast."

"Sorry about that. I was up late last night." I felt like I was telling her that I had stayed out past curfew, nearly forgetting that I was a paying guest at the cottage. It was all too homey and comfortable. And Mrs. Curtis had such a motherly aura about her.

"Well, what can I get for you?" she asked.

"Oh, don't worry about it. I'd hate for you to make something just for me."

"Well, why not? You are the only guest right now," she said.

"I am?" I looked around as if I'd find some people hiding behind the curtains or something.

"Yes," she said, opening the refrigerator and peering inside. "I'm afraid business has been slower lately."

"Oh, that's too bad. Well, I'm sure it will pick up." This was just something to say. I had no idea how tourism worked and if things would pick up. I could only hope they would.

"Yes, me too," she said.

After making me a cranberry turkey sandwich that was one of the best things I'd ever eaten, I headed back up to the room to figure out what I was going to do. I needed to see Miss Anna Cate, but I kept procrastinating. It felt like it would be too hard and too final.

Around two in the afternoon, after going back and forth in my head, I realized that this whole trip wasn't going to work and called the airline to arrange to change my ticket. I got all the way to the end of the process, and even had my credit card out to pay the change fee, but for some reason I couldn't pull the trigger. So I canceled the changes and decided that I'd give it another day before doing anything.

Not long after hanging up with the airline, my phone beeped with a text from Andy asking me if I wanted to meet up after he was done with work. We agreed on a time, and I finally had something to do. At least there was Andy.

It was weird to be getting texts from him again. Back in high school that was our main mode of communication. Sometimes we'd stay up late into the night texting each other, using those awful flip phones that took forever to type anything out. But it was new and it was novel. At least for us it was. He was the only one I had that kind of relationship with back then. There were a lot of things we did together that I didn't do with anyone else. Like during the summer, we used to sneak out of our houses and play at night. I think our parents knew but pretended like they didn't. It was innocent fun, anyway.

I got ready and grabbed my camera, which I had brought with me but had yet to take any pictures with, and headed into town. Maybe I'd stop by the falls and snap some pictures. It was one of my favorite places to take pictures. And then, of course, I'd manipulate the photo, taking the bright colors out and making it darker, but still beautiful. Just beautiful in a different way.

My first stop was the bakery in the grocery store where Mrs. Mitchem was busy decorating a couple of cakes. One for a birthday and one for a Christmas party. I snapped a couple pictures of her creations—not to manipulate and change like I usually did, but to have for myself. I had a few pictures of the bakery when I worked there, but they were mostly of me and Piper acting like idiots, or Andy goofing around.

I also reloaded up on sugar cookies, because why not. I was going to have to go on an all veggie diet when I got back to San Francisco anyway. Might as well enjoy myself while I was here.

I still had an hour before I was meeting up with Andy, and I'd been putting my visit to Miss Anna Cate off long enough. It wasn't that I didn't want to see her—I did, with all my heart—but I worried that seeing her sick would be too hard. And I was also slightly nervous that she, too, wouldn't recognize me. I didn't think my heart could handle that. I'd always felt like Miss Anna Cate got me—that she saw through my high school goth exterior and right into my soul. She never judged me, she just loved me, which was exactly what I needed back then. I still needed it.

I started walking over to her small house, not too far from the community center where she volunteered most of her time. I took pictures here and there as I went. It was a nice day, only a slight chill in the air, which added to the ambiance of this little town. I was wearing off-white skinny jeans with a light beige cable knit sweater and cropped heel boots in chocolate brown.

I'd actually taken a little extra time getting ready because I had the time, and I also wanted Andy to see me looking like a normal person and not in my PJs. It was odd that I wanted to make an effort—I mean, this was Andy, my best guy friend growing up. He'd seen me at my absolute worst.

I stood at the doorway readying my hand to knock, feeling butterflies doing back flips and somersaults in my stomach. I was so nervous to see what lay beyond that door. How sick was she? There was only one way to find out.

I heard the rattling of the doorknob and then saw it turn as the door creaked open.

"Miss Anna Cate?" I asked as the door opened wider.

There she stood in a soft pink robe, silky white pajamas, and bunny slippers on her feet. She looked tired and a bit worn around the edges—her face was slightly swollen, as were her hands—but for the most part, she was still Miss Anna Cate. I felt sudden relief at the sight of her. Seeing that she was still whole gave me hope, and I felt emotions trying to push out from behind my eyes, but I held them in. Not that Miss Anna Cate couldn't handle my feelings—she'd always been a shoulder to cry on when I was younger—but because I felt like I wanted to be strong for her.

"Well," she said, putting her hands on her hips. "If it isn't Miss London Walsh standing on my doorstep."

She opened her arms and I carefully put my arms around her, not wanting to exacerbate any pain she might be having. But when she hugged me tight, I figured I didn't need to be so cautious, so I reciprocated the hug, holding on to her tightly.

"Let me look at you," she said as we pulled out of the hug. She grabbed one of my hands as if I might fly away if she let me go, and she stood back looking me up and down. "Don't you look lovely, my dear," she said. "You're all grown up."

It was then that a tear did escape and travel down the side of my face. She recognized me. And I didn't think anyone had ever called me a grownup. I was constantly being told to "grow up" by my family, and even I didn't think I was making grown-up choices these days.

"Come in, let's have some tea," she said as I walked in the door.

She gestured for me to take a seat in a dark gray wingback chair in her living room while she clanked and shuffled around the kitchen, humming to herself all the while. I looked around the space and memories of being here came back to me. Practicing for the pageant with Piper, gathered around the upright piano while Miss Anna Cate accompanied us. Andy sitting on the couch making silly faces at us while we tried to practice. The piano was still in the same spot. The cover was even open, as if someone had played it recently. So many memories were made here, with Piper and with Miss Anna Cate. The melancholy feeling was back again.

"Here you go," she said, setting down a tray on the coffee table that filled the space between the couch and the chairs. "So, tell me about you." She settled into the couch across from me, pulling a blanket over herself as she did. I felt a twinge of sadness run through me. The room was stifling hot to me, and yet she was cold.

"I'm doing pretty good," I said.

"Well, now, I'm sure you are doing more than that," she said, her head angling to the side, her face filled with skepticism.

"Yes, well . . ." I trailed off, twiddling with my camera strap.

"Still taking pictures, I see," she said with a nod toward the contraption sitting in my lap.

"Yep," I said simply.

"That's wonderful," she smiled. "You always had a knack for that. I still have the one you did for me," she turned her head in the direction of the framed picture I'd done of the falls. I'd given it to her for a Christmas present one year. I was touched to see it still hanging there on the wall.

"So, now, tell me about you."

So I did. I filled her in on the life of London Walsh. I didn't try to sugarcoat things or leave anything out, because this was Miss Anna Cate. She loved me for me, and there was no need for pretense around her. I told her about Phoenix and San Francisco, about my life since I left Christmas Falls.

"That's too bad about your parents," she said, her lips forming a frown after I updated her on my family.

"Yeah," I agreed.

"Well, sounds like you've had quite the ride," she said.

I half-laughed. "Yes, I suppose." It was kind of a ride, I guess. An unintentional one.

"Isn't that what life's all about, though? Enjoying the ride?"

I smiled. How Miss Anna Cate could be so positive was always amazing to me. She was widowed since before I ever met her and never married again, and she never was able to have children. Her children, she had said on many occasions, were her students.

"Miss Anna Cate?" I asked, pulling my brows inward.

"What's going on with you?"

She batted the question away with her hand, as if it were no big deal. As if it wasn't about her at all.

She sighed. "My kidneys have given out and I need a new one."

"Oh," I said, feeling hope start to take root. There were options, then.

She held out a hand, as if she knew what I was thinking. "I'm no young thing," she said, her lips forming into a small smile. "Which means, I'm not at the top of the donor list."

"Oh," I said again, this time my "oh" sounded more as if that hope that had just taken flight had fallen to the road and been run over. Twice.

"Whatever happens is meant to be. I've had a good ride," she said, her head turning to look out the window that was bringing in most of the light to the room. I nodded in response as the lump in my throat wouldn't allow me to do much more than that.

I wanted to tell her that she shouldn't give up hope. That maybe a miracle could happen. But I'm not sure I could have gotten it out without crying and I was pretty sure she didn't need me blubbering all over her right now.

"Well," she said, clasping her hands together and placing them in her lap. Her tone indicated she was ready to move on from that discussion. "Now that I have you here, we'll need to practice for the pageant." Her lips curled up into a bright smile.

"Right," I said after taking in a deep breath to try and pull myself together. "About that . . ." I started.

"Oh no, you aren't going to break an old dying

woman's heart by telling me you can't be there, are you?" She raised her eyebrows high, giving me her best disapproving look. See? Now that's how you properly guilt someone in a passive-aggressive way. My mother could take a few lessons from Miss Anna Cate.

"Well," I said. "I mean, I didn't exactly think this whole trip through. I just hopped on a plane."

"And I'm grateful you did. And now that you're here, you can stay and sing in the pageant. We need your voice—the community center needs you."

"Is Piper going to sing?"

"I believe so."

This made my heard beat up. Did Piper want to sing with me? Would it be weird?

I fidgeted with the strap on my camera, rolling it between my thumb and index finger.

"Well, she could sing it," I said. Piper had the better singing voice between the two of us.

"No, it has to be both of you. I need you two there," she said. I could tell by her tone that she wouldn't be taking no for an answer. Only Miss Anna Cate would be able to get Piper and me back together and have us sing in the Christmas pageant. No one else would have been able to pull this off.

I sat there, still twiddling the camera strap in my fingers, coming up with all the reasons I should go and only thinking of one reason to stay—for her. It was an easy decision, she'd done so much for me, of course I would stay for her.

"I'll stay," I said, giving her a closed mouth smile.

She clapped her hands together. "Yes! I knew you

wouldn't let me down. Now," she said giving me a jovial smile, "let's celebrate by having some tea."

"So, what are you going to do for the next ten days while you're in the Falls?" Andy asked as we walked out of Tinsel's coffee shop, both bundled up in our winter coats, hats, and scarves, and both carrying a piping hot cup of hot chocolate. I was going to get caramel brulée coffee—one of the specialties of the shop—but then I saw the hot chocolate on the menu and it reminded me of Piper, so I got that instead. I was really missing her; memories of her were everywhere in this town. At least for me they were. And I was regretting even more how everything had ended.

"Well, I'm counting on you to keep me entertained," I said, bumping his arm with mine.

"I'm at your service," he said, giving me a small bow.

We started walking toward the falls, not even acknowledging the decision to go there—it was unspoken, just like old times.

We crossed the street and passed the fire department and the community center on our way to the path that took us to the falls. I stopped and took it all in once we got to end of the path and also tried to catch my breath—my heart was pumping overtime to keep me warm. The falls, though, were worth any amount of cold. I mean, I'd seen this waterfall more times than I could probably count, and yet, seeing it again nearly took my breath away. Or perhaps I still couldn't catch my breath. It was odd, but I felt like the falls were even prettier now. Maybe because I could see it through eyes of appreciation, rather than those of a teenager who took everything for granted.

"I wish I had my camera," I said, regretting the fact that I'd left my camera back at the cottage.

"You brought it with you?" Andy asked as we walked over to the bench and took a seat, sitting close to each other to share body heat.

"Of course," I said.

"Some things never change," he said, and I caught his smiling profile as he looked out on the falls.

Once upon a time, I almost always had my camera with me. It was my constant companion back when I lived here. Honestly though, this past year it had stayed more and more in the black equipment bag that I kept in the closet at my apartment.

"Speaking of things that never change," I said, tugging my hat more firmly over my ears for warmth. "This is exactly how I remembered it." I gestured toward the falls with a dip of my chin.

"Yep," Andy nodded. "Still the same."

"I kind of love that about this place."

"Me too."

"So," I asked, feeling reluctant and not sure why— this was Andy, for heaven's sake. "About Christmas—"

"You're coming to our house. I already asked my mom," he said. "She's excited to see you."

"But how did you know I'd stay?"

"I just had a feeling," he said. Stretching his arm up and putting it around my shoulders, he pulled me into him, giving me a side hug. He left his arm there and it felt good as I snuggled into him. I rested my head on his chest and could hear his quick heartbeat and wondered if his body was also working hard to keep him warm. I was starting to feel all kinds of warm right now, sitting next to Andy.

"Your arms aren't quite as bony as the last time we sat here," I said, remembering the last time we sat in this very spot. It was right before my family moved to Phoenix. Our last hurrah—we grabbed ice cream and came up to the falls. I remembered feeling extra sad to leave Andy that day, but ready to go someplace else, to try something new, and to get away from the drama with Piper.

It was so silly and we should have resolved it then, but Piper and I were dumb teenagers. It was one of my biggest regrets in life. Would either of our lives be different if we had worked things out? At the very least, we would have kept in touch and I wouldn't have had to hear about her life from someone else.

"I'm pretty buff now." Andy smirked.

"I wouldn't go that far," I said, and I felt his arm tighten around me as he flexed his muscles.

I reached up and felt the taut arm bulging beneath the sleeve of his wool coat. Not too shabby, actually. But I couldn't tell him that.

"Meh, I've felt better," I said, and I laid my head on his shoulder, which was also a lot less bony than last time.

"Shut up," he said. I felt him lean his head toward me and expected him to rest his head on mine. Instead he placed a kiss on the top of my head. As we sat here by the falls, drinking hot chocolate, all felt right in the world.

Six

THE NEXT DAY WAS FRIDAY, and already having made plans with Andy for that evening, I decided that I wasn't going to spend the day locked up in my room. So what if only two people had recognized me in the entire town. At least they were the two most important people.

I ate breakfast at the cottage. Mrs. Curtis made me pancakes topped with fresh berries and whipped cream, and during breakfast, Mr. Curtis schooled me in the way to pronounce poinsettia. Apparently, the correct pronunciation is poin-set-ee-ah. Not point-set-uh as everyone says it. I had no idea if this was true, but he was very determined about it.

After I left the cottage, I decided I would go see Mrs. Mitchem and ask if she needed any help in the bakery. I'd never been one to sit around, I liked having something to do. Sometimes being lazy and resting was a good thing, but I'd found that lately sitting around made me contemplate my life choices and I really didn't want to go there.

I went straight back to the bakery and, after an awkward conversation where Mrs. Mitchem tried to explain to me that they already had help and couldn't afford to pay me, we got it squared away that I was there solely on a volunteer basis, and a temporary one at that. Like, just for the day, temporary.

She was thrilled to have me help and even said I was an answer to a prayer—they had been working around the clock to fill all of the holiday orders. I spent the rest of the afternoon baking and frosting (and eating) sugar cookies. I asked if I could take a few for Andy and got a knowing look from Mrs. Mitchem.

"You still hanging out with the Broll boy? He's back in town?" she asked as she rolled out the dough for cinnamon rolls. She was wearing a hot pink apron with black polka-dot ruffles. I had borrowed a lovely Christmas tree-covered one. It went nicely with my black leggings and soft pink tunic sweater.

"He's back in town, yes. But this is the first I've seen or heard from him since we moved away," I said.

"Well, isn't that a shame," she shook her head. "You kids and all your Twitters and stuff. You'd think you'd be able to keep in touch better."

"You'd think," I said. The truth was, I had purposely not kept in touch. That was the sad part of it.

"Anything going on with that Andy that I should know about?" she asked with a double eyebrow raise. "I mean, y'all were quite cozy in high school."

"Andy?" I scoffed. "Nope. Just friends. We were never more than that."

"Really?" She pulled her eyebrows in and squinted her eyes. "You sure seemed like ya had something."

I supposed from an outside view we probably did look like more than friends. But it had never been that way with us. Sure, we'd snuggled up together on his bed while watching a show in his room, or lain out under the stars at night in the summertime. Sometimes we held hands for no reason. But it was never more. On the rare occasion I had a date in high school, I did find myself often wanting to be with Andy instead. But only because he was one of my best friends; it was easy with him. There was no getting to know you part, nothing expected of me. I could just be me with Andy. I felt that way even now, even after eight years of not seeing him. There was so much comfort in my friendship with Andy.

"Well, maybe now that you're older there might be something?" Mrs. Mitchem asked with a touch of insinuation in her tone.

I scoffed. "Um, no. Andy and I . . . no."

"And why's that?"

"Because we're just friends."

"Well," she gave me a half-shrug. "Friendship is the best foundation for romance to bloom."

I rolled my eyes because Mrs. Mitchem had always tried to match up everyone back in the day. I was happy to see she hadn't let that go, even if it was directed at me. Misdirected, really.

I finished up at the bakery in time to go back to the cottage, take a shower, and get ready to hang out with

Andy. This trip—even with its poor start—was turning out to be just what I had hoped for, and what I'd needed. After seeing Andy and Miss Anna Cate and spending time at the bakery with a misguided Mrs. Mitchem, it was feeling more like the home I'd romanticized in my head.

"You look lovely," Andy said as I met him outside the cottage. I was wearing dark blue skinny jeans, a flowy, button-up, deep green top and knee-high charcoal-gray boots. I had my cream peacoat in hand and my gloves, scarf, and hat tucked in my purse just in case I needed them.

"Not too shabby yourself," I said, motioning with my hand at him. He was wearing jeans and his wool coat was open to a soft-looking navy-blue v-neck sweater over a white collared shirt. We both had done some changing since high school.

"What happened to your eyes?" I asked when I saw that his eyes were red and irritated behind his black-rimmed glasses.

"Oh that," he said, reaching up and rubbing one of them with his finger. "Just some allergies, I think."

"In the middle of winter?"

"Yep."

"Really?" I took a challenging stance, leaning back on my left leg, my right foot pointed slightly out, my arms folded.

"Yes, allergies," he confirmed. "Maybe I'm allergic to people from San Francisco."

"Oh yes, I've heard that's an actual thing," I said, trying to hold back a smile.

"Oh, it's real." He did a very good serious face when he wanted to. "Is there anything I can take for it?"

"The best thing to do is to keep hanging out with the person so that you can adjust to the allergy."

"And this diagnosis is from a professional, then?"

"Yes," I said, giving him a mock-serious look. "It's definitely from a professional."

He leaned in and kissed me on the cheek. "Come on," he said. "Let's get out of here."

He grabbed my hand as we started off. It was only meant to be a friendly gesture on Andy's part, I'm sure, but for some reason my heart did a little thump when his hand touched mine. Which was preposterous. I wrote it off as a palpitation from all the sugar I had consumed that day. Which reminded me . . .

"Hold on," I said, letting go of his hand. "I forgot something. I need to run back upstairs and grab it."

I hurried up to my room, waving at Mr. Curtis as I went by, grabbed the sugar cookies, and hurried back to Andy. When I got outside, I found him talking to a redheaded woman who was dressed in a police uniform, and it looked to be a friendly conversation. I couldn't place her from when I lived here before; she didn't look familiar at all. She was tall, with shoulder length red hair and freckles . . . the cute kind of freckles. She also looked strong—like she could kick my butt, strong.

"We should definitely get together sometime," I heard Andy say as I approached. I noticed that he had quite the smile on his face.

"I'd like that," she said, returning the smile. And was that a wink?

"Hi," I said as I approached them.

"Oh, hey," Andy said like he hadn't seen me just two minutes ago. "This is London Walsh," he gestured toward me with his hand, his eyes still on the redhead.

"Hi, London," redheaded police officer put her hand out for me to shake, which I did.

"This is Katrina Hutchins, she's new to Christmas Falls—or newer, I guess. How long have you been here?" Andy asked.

"Just over a year," she said, focusing solely on Andy, a flirtatious smile on her face.

"That's cool." I did a weird head-bobbing thing.

"We met a couple of weeks back at the bookstore," Andy said to me, pointing in the direction of The Enchanted Attic—the lone bookstore in Christmas Falls.

"Hey, Andrew, did you end up liking the book you bought?" Katrina asked. I really didn't like this use of his full name. It just wasn't him.

"I did," he said, nodding his head.

She asked him another question, but I had tuned out because there was suddenly something swirling in my stomach. Something off-putting. I instantly didn't like this woman, and I had no idea why. Maybe I had suddenly developed a bout of clairvoyance and could tell she was up to no good. But that wasn't it. She looked normal—she was probably lovely. Plus, I had never been clairvoyant in my life. In fact, more often than not, it was better for me to ignore my gut feeling all together.

"I'll be in touch," Andy said as Katrina with the stupid red hair turned away from us and headed toward the downtown area.

"She seemed nice," I said, even though I still had a weird feeling about her.

"She is," he said simply.

"Are you going to hang out with her or something?" The words were out of my mouth before I could stop myself.

"Like go on a date?" he asked.

I shrugged, playing it cool. "Yeah."

"I don't know," he shrugged back. "Maybe. Why? Feeling a little jealous, Walsh?" he said, a playful smile on his face. He used to say that to me all the time when we were in high school.

"No way," I retorted, squinting my eyes at him.

"Don't be jealous," Andy said with a conniving smile. "There's plenty of me to go around."

I slapped him lightly on the stomach with the back of my hand. "I'm not jealous."

But that swirling in my stomach just then . . . Was that . . . jealousy? It kind of felt like it. I mean, maybe it was . . . only because he said he would entertain me while I was in town. Yes. It was definitely that. And I didn't want this chick swooping in and taking him away while I was here. Of course, that was it. Because this was Andy, after all. My friend Andy. My F-R-I-E-N-D.

But then Mrs. Mitchem's words came to mind. *Friendship is the best foundation for romance to bloom.* I pushed them out because she was obviously a complete nut job. I had half a mind to never go to the bakery again, if it wasn't for those darn sugar cookies.

Shaking all that off, I handed him the small box of cookies. "For you," I said.

"Is this what I think it is?" he asked, his eyes moving from the box to me, then back to the box.

"Yep," I said as he took it from me.

He opened it. "Oh, yes," he said with a lust-filled voice. "Mrs. Mitchem's sugar cookies. I think I've died and gone to heaven."

"Have you had any since you've been back?" I asked.

"Not yet," he said, picking one up and taking a huge bite. "Oh, my gosh," he said through a mouth full of sugar cookie.

"Right?" I asked, reaching in the box to grab one for myself, my mouth actually drooling at the thought of eating one. But Andy shut the lid before I could. "Hey," I protested.

"Didn't you get these for me?" he asked, angling the box away from me as I tried to reach for it.

"Yes, but you could share, you brat," I said, trying harder to get it from him and failing. His arms were longer and stronger than mine.

"I might share," he said. "But I'll have to see if you're worthy of a cookie."

I rolled my eyes at him. "And how might I go about proving that?"

"We'll just have to see how the evening goes." He turned, holding out the arm that wasn't holding the cookies, and I slid my arm through, my hand sitting in the crook of his elbow, and we started walking across the street.

"Where are we going?" I asked as he led me.

"You'll see," he said with a wink.

"I hate surprises."

"I know."

He pulled keys out of his pocket and hit the unlock button on his key fob. Immediately a black SUV that was parked on the street only a few feet away lit up, flashing yellow lights at us. He escorted me to the passenger side and I climbed in, annoyed that I didn't know where we were going, still feeling strange about how I responded to the redheaded police officer. I mean, there was nothing going on here. Andy and I were friends—we had always been just friends. He was free to date anyone he wanted because we weren't dating. Even pretty redheaded police officers.

Why did that thought make me so annoyed? Maybe she was evil. Maybe I actually was psychic this time. Or maybe Mrs. Mitchem had cast some weird spell on me. Stupid Mrs. Mitchem and her crazy thoughts.

"Buckle up," he said as he got in the car, carefully placing the box of cookies on the back seat.

"Where are we going?" I asked again, sounding more annoyed than I truly was. Actually, I was annoyed, but not at him. I was irritated with myself.

"Pigeon Forge," he said.

I let out a quick gasp. "Pigeon Forge . . . you mean we're going to Winterfest?"

"Yep," he nodded once, a big smile on his face.

I jumped around in my seat. I loved Winterfest—it was one of my favorite things about living near the Smoky Mountains. The lights, the Christmas decor, the carolers, I loved it all. I only wished I had brought my camera with me, but I left it back at the cottage because I'd always been terrible at taking pictures at night.

"I like," I said as I beamed at him. I felt my heart do a strange jumping thing when we made eye contact and he smiled back at me. It was like something flickered between us. What the heck was that? I turned away from him and looked straight ahead out the windshield. This whole spirit of the holidays and Christmas Falls was clearly getting to me.

Seven

"ARE YOU FOR REAL?" I asked, playfully hitting Andy on the arm.

"I am," he said, dipping his chin to his chest once.

We'd had fun conversation on the drive up to Pigeon Forge, slipping back into old Andy and London. My heart, thankfully, stopped doing that weird jumping, and my brain stopped conjuring up odd thoughts—and I even wondered if I'd had a bout of temporary insanity back there. Because this was Andy, after all.

We parked and Andy had to practically drag me over to the back part of the street behind where most of the Winterfest celebration was going on. I wanted to get right into it—but he apparently had other plans.

"Are you serious?" I asked. Still not believing where we were right now.

"Yes," he said, adding a chuckle. "I told you I'd make it worth it if you stayed."

I looked up at the beautiful white horse harnessed to a lovely old-fashioned carriage that was decorated with Christmas lights. A coachman with a cowboy hat and one of those handlebar mustaches was seated on the perch, waiting for us to hop in.

"After you," Andy said, helping me up into the carriage.

Once we were seated with a large blanket over us to keep us warm, we took off. It was a slow pace, ideal for us to take in the Christmas spirit that was everywhere. The ambiance, the lights, the company . . . it was perfect. I felt giddy, like Christmas had literally taken over my body. This was *so* what I needed right now.

"So, is it all you dreamed it would be?" he asked, leaning into me. We were quite cozy under the blanket, leg pressed against leg, arm against arm.

"It's amazing," I said. Then I realized what he'd asked me. Once upon a time, this *was* my dream, to ride in a horse-driven carriage at Winterfest. "You remembered," I said, turning my face toward him to find him looking at me. My heart did that strange jumping thing again. Maybe I needed to get that checked by a doctor.

"Of course," he said, his lips turning up into a small smile. "I remember that time we came here with our families, and you pointed to one of these carriages and said you wanted to have a ride, but your mom was not into it and your dad was mad about something."

"I remember that night," I said, bobbing my head as the memories came rushing back. My dad was mad because my mom had been complaining the entire night, ruining the evening for all of us. It hadn't ruined the evening for me, though, because I was with Andy. And things were always fun with Andy. Even though I hadn't thought about it in years, suddenly I remembered everything about that night.

Andy looked away from me and out into the street in front of us. "I remember thinking to myself, someday I was going to take you here." He reached up and put his arm around me, and I rested my cheek on his shoulder.

I sighed, a big, contented sigh. "Thank you," I said, willing the fluttering butterflies in my lower belly to chill out. What was wrong with my body?

"You're welcome."

The night was magical. We stopped to get hot chocolate to warm us after the carriage ride. Carolers, dressed like characters out of a Dickens' novel, serenaded the streets, the perfect accompaniment to the light show provided by the storefronts.

"So, listen," he said as we were driving back to Christmas Falls.

"Yeah?"

"I may have crossed a line," he said.

"What line?" I asked, wondering what the apprehension in his voice was for.

"Well, I told Piper I would set up a time for you to get together," he said.

"You did what?"

"Is that okay? She wants to see you."

"Oh," I said. I wasn't mad—not at all. I'd actually been missing Piper so much it almost hurt. There were so many memories of her—of us—around this town. How could I not?

"What do you think?"

"I think . . . it's a great idea," I said.

"You do?" he questioned, turning his face briefly to mine to see if I was bluffing.

"Sure," I said. "I want to see Piper." Especially before the pageant. We needed to bury the hatchet before then, for us and for Miss Anna Cate.

"Okay," he said. "How about Sunday? Does that work?"

"Uh, let me check my schedule," I said, picking up my smart phone and pretending to look at it. "I think I'm free."

"Are you worried at all about seeing her?" he asked, ignoring my sarcasm.

"Yeah. Kind of." Actually, it was more than kind of. Especially when memories and feelings came swirling back as I allowed myself to go back to that time in my head. I had pushed those memories out, so you'd think they'd be foggy—but they weren't. I could even remember what I was wearing that day everything changed, even what Piper was wearing.

"You never told me what happened," Andy said.

I sighed, debating in my mind if it was even worth telling him, worth bringing up those feelings. They were going to get dredged up anyway. Might as well rip the Band-Aid off now.

"Remember Tad Johnson?"

"That moron?" he said, and I knew he'd say that like I knew the sun would rise. Andy hated Tad and Tad hated Andy.

"Yep. The very one." I shook my head at Andy, chuckling to myself, because even after all these years, he still had the same response when hearing his name. Tad *was* a moron. Actually, he was handsome and vivacious, and every girl in school wanted to date him. But he was also a moron.

"What about him?" he asked.

"Piper liked him—like a lot. Remember? She'd spend forever writing his name in fancy lettering in her notebooks."

Andy shook his head at that, because of course he wouldn't remember. I was the only one privy to that information.

"Anyway, apparently, he either knew that she liked him and was just a jerk, or he actually had a thing for me, because he tried to kiss me at the after-graduation party at the Cooks' house, and remember Brittany?"

"Ah yes, the resident mean girl," he said.

"Yeah, that's the one. She caught a picture just at the right moment and showed it to Piper."

"Oh," he said, drawing out the word, understanding dawning.

"Yeah. It didn't look good from any angle. And when I tried to tell Piper what happened, she wouldn't even talk to me. You remember that day," I said, and looked over to see him nodding. "I was crying my eyes out and you were really sweet." I reached over and squeezed his arm.

Andy had been great. It had hurt to think that Piper would write me off like that—without even listening to me. I mean, she had liked Tad for a long time before that, and Piper was so pretty, it was hard to believe that he'd never tried to date her. And to be honest, when he kissed me, for a moment—a split second—I had felt . . . special. Even though a split second later I pushed him away and yelled at him. I'd always felt like Piper was the prettier one, and everyone always talked about all the amazing things she was going to do after high school—she was voted most likely to succeed, after all. And I was just me. Voted most likely to be sorted into Slytherin. Which was ridiculous. I mean, clearly I was meant for Ravenclaw at the very least.

I'd gone directly to Andy's house after the whole debacle, and he put a boney arm around me while I sobbed. I remembered, once I was done crying on Andy, looking down at my wrist and seeing that friendship bracelet—the one London and I had made at the community center and Miss Anna Cate had recited that poem to go with it – *Ties That Bind*, it was called. I loved that bracelet and never took it off. But when I looked down at it that day, something snapped. I ripped it off and threw it on the ground somewhere in Andy's backyard.

"Anyway, we moved away two weeks later."

"And you never talked to her again after that?" he asked.

I shrugged one shoulder. "I didn't think she wanted to talk to me. Plus, I'd moved across the country."

I had planned to keep in touch with Piper, with Andy, with Miss Anna Cate. Andy, Piper, and I were all going away to college soon—we knew that our lives would be heading different ways anyway. My move was just faster since I missed our last summer together.

When things went so wrong with Piper, I sort of followed my mom's lead when we moved. She wanted a fresh start—a clean break from our old lives. To start anew. I wanted that too, thinking it was the answer to everything. I was so angry about how things had ended with Piper. Deciding not to even think about it was my best defense at the time.

My parents bought a house in Phoenix that was nothing like the one they had in Christmas Falls. They got rid of all our old furniture and decorated the new house to fit in better with their "new lives." I went away to college, and it wasn't long before Christmas Falls was a thing of the past.

Plus, Piper never tried to contact me. Not that she really could have—I changed my number to an Arizona area code because my parents were footing the bill and wanted us to all get new numbers. I realized that I was going to have to be the one to reach out to her, and I avoided it long enough that I just moved on. Well, I tried to move on. All of it would sneak up on me sometimes, and I'd feel so much regret that I'd work extra hard to shove it away again. Funny how the past did that.

Andy pulled up in front of Poinsettia Cottage and put the car in park. He turned to look at me. "Can I ask you something?" The serious look on his face made my stomach drop.

"Yeah?"

"Why didn't you ever call me?" The look on his face,

the hurt that was there, made my heart feel like it was breaking.

I let out a shaky breath. "Andy," I shook my head. "I meant to. I didn't mean not to. I just . . . I don't know."

I looked down at my hands in my lap, feeling ashamed. Andy had been one of my closest friends and didn't deserve the way I handled everything back then. It wasn't intentional, us losing contact. More like a byproduct of what had transpired with Piper.

"I'm really, really sorry."

He looked at me, his eyes sad, and I braced myself for what was going to come out of his mouth next.

"I'm sorry too. But I'm afraid . . ." he paused to give me a sullen look. "I'm afraid I won't be able to share my sugar cookies with you. You don't deserve them."

A slow smile crept across his face, and I chuckled. I also felt butterflies swirling around in my stomach—the excited kind. I had Andy back, and hopefully soon, Piper.

Christmas Falls was suddenly feeling quite magical.

Eight

THAT NIGHT AFTER ANDY DROPPED me off and I felt happier than I had in a long time, I had a dream. It was one of *those* dreams. And, of course, it was about Andy.

It was the kind of dream you don't want to wake up from because it felt like it was out of a romance movie. There were lovey-dovey words and kissing and touching and everything was perfect. When I woke up, I felt elated, and then I felt like I was going to be sick. First Mrs. Mitchem, then my heart and stomach . . . now my subconscious was in on this thing.

I needed to get over it, and fast, because before I got out of the car last night, Andy had remembered that his mom invited me to come over to dinner the next day. I, of course, told him yes because you didn't turn down food made by Andy's mom, and because it meant more time with Andy.

I also really wanted to see his parents, to see their house, and the one next to it—the one I had grown up in.

I hadn't gone by yet, and I had no idea why I was putting it off. Maybe it would be too sad to see it. Well, I was going to find out tonight. Unless I called and canceled, citing that romantic dream I couldn't stop thinking about. Stupid subconscious.

"You're up early," Mrs. Curtis said as I came down the stairs. I had actually been up before seven, but lay in bed replaying the stupid dream I'd had, and the night before and the carriage ride. So many thoughts swirling around in my head.

"Yes, lots to do today," I said, and then mentally slapped myself. Why would I say that? I had nothing to do except for dinner tonight at Andy's parents' house.

"Oh, well, then you'll need something to eat," Mrs. Curtis said with a wink. Today, rather than sit in the kitchen, she urged me into the dining room. Odd of her to want to dirty another room since I was the only guest, but I followed her directions.

The dining room was filled with poinsettias, some real, but mostly fake ones. There was a lot of ornate décor and antiques around the room. And tons of pictures on the walls—older pictures of what I figured were ancestors of the Curtis family. I loved it all. The Curtis home was what I wanted. Maybe not so cluttered, and definitely not the bed and breakfast thing—I couldn't cook and therefore would only serve boxed cereal or microwavable oatmeal—but the hominess of it all. The feeling that people had lived here, that history had happened here. I don't think I could find that in San Francisco. Sure, there was history there—tons of it. But nothing like this. Small Southern towns had so much charm and warmth.

Maybe someday I would have a home like this. A place to bring my future children home to. Little Kingston and Ireland. I wasn't planning on following that tradition, but if I did I would make sure my children were conceived in the coolest of places.

I lay on my bed after eating the Belgian waffle Mrs. Curtis had made me. My belly was full, and I was feeling something I hadn't felt in a long while. Content. And it wasn't just the waffle. It was the holidays, it was Christmas Falls, it was Miss Anna Cate, it was Andy. It was a lot Andy. I felt like my brain was filled with some big marquee with the word "Andy" in huge lights flashing repeatedly. "Andy! Andy! Andy!"

Why, when I thought of his name, would my stomach do all kinds of flipping things? This was new and foreign, and I felt like a teenager. That dream had quite the effect on me. Or perhaps it was just the waffle. I could hope that was the reason.

To clear my head, I grabbed my camera and took a walk to the falls, where I spent the next couple of hours taking pictures of the falls themselves, the trees and the foliage surrounding it, the bench, all the little details that I never wanted to forget. Who knew when I'd be back here again?

Using a wide-angle lens, I snapped a shot of the whole area. I was going to blow it up and frame it for my apartment. This time leaving it just as it was, no Photoshop tricks. It didn't need any enhancements or changes.

After I'd filled an entire memory card, I sat on the bench and contemplated life. Something I didn't do very often because, well, my life hadn't turned out at all like I'd planned. Not that it was a bad life; it just wasn't spectacular or fancy. I hadn't followed any of the dreams I had set out for myself. Dreams I had thought up years ago sitting at this same bench.

I'd had lots of dreams, but my biggest was to do something with photography. I was never quite sure what to do, but I knew if I could make money using my camera, I would be happy. I planned to go to college at some fancy art school and carve out a life where I could do something I loved. But none of that happened. Art school somehow turned into business school. Mostly because my mom convinced me that photography was a hobby and not a career. She was right, of course. Photography never amounted to much for me. But then again, neither had marketing.

I watched the water as it fell into the pool. The same journey it always took, moving out of the pool and feeding into the river that went through Christmas Falls. At least there was movement there and not a holding pattern, like with my life. Perhaps that was my problem. Maybe I'd been stuck in a holding pattern for too long, living in the same place, staying in the same kind of job.

Maybe I needed to mix things up—to do something new. Perhaps I could try a new career or something. Maybe move into a bigger apartment and find a roommate. Maybe I could join an online dating site. Okay, probably not that. But I could do something different. I could get myself out of the holding pattern I was in. Maybe I just needed a change.

"London!" Linda Broll, Andy's mom, exclaimed as she opened the door. I was standing at the doorstep feeling all kinds of unexplained nerves. What was going on with me? Maybe it was because I had just seen my old house and now Andy's, and there were so many memories here.

"Hi, Mrs. Broll—"

"Oh, call me Linda," she said. "We're all adults now."

"Okay, Linda," I stepped into the Broll home, a place where I had spent a lot of time in my youth, and into Linda's arms for a hug. She looked the same as I remembered her. She had the same hairstyle—short bob, stacked in the back—and she wore basically the same style of clothes. She was apparently still sticking with the mom jeans.

The house was the same too. A craftsman-style home with a wide front porch and heather-gray exterior with white trim and plantation shutters. The house I grew up in, the one next door, was similar on the outside, except the porch wrapped around the side of the house and it was painted white with dark gray accents. At least, that's how it was when we lived there. The new tenants had painted it a lovely shade of sea-foam green.

Before I got here, I had so badly wanted to see the inside of my old house—I had planned on asking Linda if there was any way, if she even knew the neighbors well enough. But once I saw it, and the sea-foam green color, I knew that looking inside would only serve to remind me that this was not my home anymore. It would never be my home again. I'd brought my camera, so I snapped a few pictures of it before knocking on the Brolls' door.

The inside of Andy's house was basically the same as it was before, except for a few minor decor changes. The big family picture that always hung over the fireplace in the formal living room was still there, only updated. I couldn't get over how grown up Andy's brother, Nick, looked in the picture. There they were—the four of them, standing in front of a background of beautiful green pine trees, dressed in winter clothes, snow all around them. I felt envious that the Brolls still had this kind of family, this kind of house.

"Let me look at you," Linda said, standing back and looking me over. "You know, you don't look different at all. You look like the same old London to me."

I knitted my eyebrows together. "I do?" This was a first for this trip . . . and also sounded a little fishy.

"Oh, definitely," she said, but there was something unconvincing in her tone.

"Mom," I heard Andy say from somewhere in the house. I could hear his light footfalls on the hardwood floor as he made his way to the entryway where we were.

We smiled at each other as he approached, my heart doing that weird thing it had been doing lately. But then I was taken aback when he got closer—something looked off, and it took me a moment to place it. Andy wasn't wearing his glasses. The black-rimmed frames were gone. He looked so different without them. More grown-up.

"Sorry, London," Andy said, giving his mom a look.

"What? You told me to tell her she looked the same."

She motioned with her hand at me and then in a loud whisper said, "She doesn't, by the way. I barely recognized her."

"Mom," Andy chastised her with his tone.

"Well, she doesn't," she repeated.

I chuckled quietly, my shoulders shaking as I did. "It's okay," I said to Andy. "Thanks for trying."

"You look wonderful, though," Linda said. "I love what you've done with your hair."

"Thank you," I said, instinctively reaching up and tugging on a lock of it.

"Is that Miss London I hear?" Andy's dad said as he came out of the office that was just behind us. Bart Broll was a tall man, he and Andy were about the same height, but Bart's build was much brawnier than Andy. He was a big man, broad shoulders, thick forearms, and had always been in pretty good shape back when we were neighbors. Now there appeared to be the beginnings of a beer belly. He also hadn't changed his style; he wore a plaid button-down shirt and jeans.

"Now, London, don't you look exactly the same as the last time we saw you. I mean, *exactly*," he said, giving me a wink.

"Never mind, Dad," Andy said with an eye roll. He shook his head at his parents, "You both are the worst actors ever."

"Well maybe if you'd given us some warning that London had turned into this gorgeous young lady," his father said, putting an arm around me and giving me a side hug.

"Good to see you, Mr. Broll," I said, feeling my heart warm just being with this family again.

"Ah, call me Bart, darlin'," he said.

We moved the party to the family room where the Christmas tree was all set up and matching decor was on practically every surface. Linda Broll did not skimp on the Christmas decorations. I think it was against the law in Christmas Falls to be a minimalist when it came to decorating. And nothing had changed as far as that was concerned.

Andy's parents asked me a ton of questions about my family and how they were doing. My stomach took a turn when I saw their expressions after I told them about my parents' impending divorce. I wasn't even sure I should be talking about it. I had only found out five days ago myself. Part of me hoped they would figure it out—maybe work it out.

I found myself feeling rather melancholy when I realized that I might no longer have what Andy had. Not that I ever did—my family had never been as close as Andy's. My parents were definitely never as lovey-dovey as his. Bart and Linda's PDA had been a constant bane of Andy's existence growing up. I loved to tease him about it. Now, though, I appreciated that as we sat there talking, Bart had his arm around Linda, and she had her hand on his leg.

After catching up for a while, Linda excused herself to go finish making dinner and Andy and I made our way upstairs to his bedroom.

"LEAVE THE DOOR OPEN," his mom yelled up at us as we went upstairs.

I started laughing, covering my mouth so she couldn't hear me, because the look on Andy's face was killing me. He looked like he was going to strangle something. "*Mom*," he said her name through gritted teeth.

"YOU KNOW THE RULES," she yelled.

"I'm moving out next week," he said quietly to me.

"ANDREW ALAN BROLL, YOU WILL NOT MOVE OUT OF THIS HOUSE UNTIL AFTER CHRISTMAS!" she yelled up at him. "YOU PROMISED!"

"How did she hear you?" I asked.

"You forget, the woman has superpower hearing," he said.

We made our way to Andy's room, and it was like being in a time capsule. It was exactly the same as the last time I was here. He still had a poster of a space shuttle on his wall (he was going to be a rocket scientist at one point and was obsessed with all things NASA). The telescope we used to look at the sky with was still in the same place near the window.

I peered out his window and could see the adjacent window that was my old room. We had many a conversation hanging out of our windows. I remembered once we tried one of those tin can phones we saw on an old movie. The kind that had the string going from one end to the other, and supposedly you could hear each other through it. Andy was determined to make it work, but we could never figure it out.

Andy plopped down on his full-size bed, lying with his arm propped underneath his head. He patted the spot next to him for me to join him. I lay down by him, feeling like the last time I was on this bed, we fit much better than we did now. Since I was still the same height and basically the same weight I was when we graduated, the changes had clearly been on his part. It was a much different Andy I was lying next to. No longer the skinny, slightly awkward boy he used to be. Now he had filled out in all the right places—broader shoulders, muscular arms. He was definitely cute in high school, but he had morphed into quite the hottie. But I wasn't going to think about that.

Being here with him now, new Andy and all that he had become, lying on his bed with him, staring up at the slanted ceiling, I was instantly taken back. I spent so much time in Andy's room—with the door open, as was the rule in the Broll house and apparently still was. So many hours here talking, teasing, and laughing.

"This is nice," Andy said. "Like old times, right?"

"Yeah, definitely," I said, turning my head toward him. "Okay, what gives?"

"Huh?"

"Your glasses?"

"What do you mean?" he said, keeping his eyes on the ceiling.

"I mean, where'd they go?"

He angled his head toward me just slightly. "I wear contacts sometimes," he said.

"Since when?" I had never seen him in anything but those black-rimmed glasses.

"Since . . . yesterday."

That got me to lift myself up on my elbow so I could get a better look at his face. "Is that why your eyes were all red last night?"

"Maybe," he said, the tips of his ears turning pink.

"Why are you wearing contacts now?"

He shrugged. "I just wanted to try them out."

"Well, I don't like them," I said, laying my head back down next to him.

"You don't?" he asked.

"No," I said. "I like the glasses better."

He chuckled to himself.

"What?" I asked him.

"It's just that Piper said you'd prefer the glasses."

I smiled. She still knew me after all these years. I couldn't wait to see her tomorrow. Andy had set us up to meet at Tinsel's coffee shop in the morning.

"It's weird being here," I said. "It's like I've gone back in time."

"Yeah, it's weird to have you here in my bed again," he said, a teasing tone in his voice.

I whacked him lightly on the thigh with the back of my hand. "You make me sound like I was some kind of tramp."

He laughed. "Like anything would have ever happened in this room with my mom around."

"Good point," I said.

We were silent again, my mind wandering. I don't know if it was the suggestive joke he'd made or just being back here again, but I found my mind traveling off into a daydream. One where the door to his room was actually shut for once, and high school me and Andy were kissing on this bed.

Now why would my crazy brain even go there? But *there*, it went. It must have been that stupid dream I had last night. I could picture it like it had really happened.

Looking like we did back in high school, our limbs intertwined as we made out. Suddenly I could feel my heart rate speed up and Andy seemed much too close. What the heck was going on with me? It was like I had no control of my body and its reactions lately.

"You okay?" Andy asked, sensing my sudden discomfort as I tried to inch myself away and put more space between us.

"Totally," I said, practically choking out the word.

"What are you thinking about?" he asked.

There was no way in hell I was going to tell him I'd just conjured up thoughts of him and me making out back when we were teenagers, which never even happened. These were new thoughts. I'd never had these thoughts in high school. At least I don't think I did.

"Just that it's nice to be back," I finally said, only half lying.

"Yeah," he agreed.

We kept our eyes on the ceiling as Andy moved his hand slightly closer to mine, lightly rubbing his pinky finger against mine, coaxing me to turn my hand toward his. And when I did, he weaved his fingers through mine. Heat traveled up the length of my arm, up my neck, and to my face. Butterflies swirled in my stomach and my heart rate, which was already running at a fairly fast pace, picked up even more speed.

Why was I reacting this way? This was not the first time I had lain next to Andy on his bed, and it was definitely not the first time he had held my hand this way—this was our thing. Our Andy and London thing. This was something we always did. Now I was back here and it suddenly felt all different, like the time and distance between us had changed things. At least for me it seemed to have changed. The marquee in my head kept flashing "Andy! Andy! Andy!"

This was not good. Not good at all. I had been trying to push the thoughts out, but there was no denying it anymore. I had . . . or rather, I was *having* more than just friendly feelings for Andy. The ruin-your-friendship kind of feelings. And I had just gotten his friendship back. I was feeling all sorts of things right now: a mix of terror, mortification, and a dash of have-I-lost-my-mind added in for good measure.

One thing was sure, there was nothing I could do about it. Not when I was only here temporarily. Even if I tried and was subsequently rejected (as was most likely going to be the case), I might ruin this entire trip—what had been, thus far, a wonderful time, all because of Andy. If I took him out of the scenario, this trip would have been awful—minus my visit with Miss Anna Cate—and I would have been on a plane back to San Francisco days ago.

This was so *not* good.

Nine

I MET PIPER WYATT THE first day of fifth grade when we lined up for recess. We were Walsh and Wyatt, respectively. And it was friend at first sight. We immediately bonded over our hatred of school lunches and the drooling, idiot boys that were in our class that year. We both had long dark brown hair and matching tween attitudes. Well, I suspected her attitude was only a reflection of mine. I was the true tween of the two of us. Piper was just . . . kind. Everyone loved her and she seemed to love everyone, minus the drooling boys in our class. But boy, did *they* love her. Piper wasn't just cute, with her perfect nose and striking blue eyes. Even at the age of ten, it was obvious she was going to be stunning. I, on the other hand, had started at nine what was going to be a very long ugly phase.

It took a while before we crossed over from friends only at school to friends that hung out after school. But when we did, we bonded even more. We had so much in common and laughed at all the same things. Even better was the fact that Andy could hang out with us and it was no big deal. Except when we wanted to talk about girl stuff. Then Andy would act like he was annoyed. But I think he actually enjoyed it, having no sisters of his own.

Piper was my confidant, my bestie. She just got me— even when I did the whole goth thing, she was all for it, telling me I looked great in anything I wore. She was my biggest cheerleader and the person I trusted most in the world.

Which is why it felt wrong that I was so full of nerves as I got ready to meet up with her the next morning. It was sad that I was feeling so edgy, but I knew it was because of what had happened the last time I saw her. Looking back, with eight years of maturity, it seemed ridiculous to end a friendship over something so trivial.

We were to meet at Tinsel's coffee shop around ten-thirty, and I had been awake for at least three hours. My mind was going a mile a minute, thinking about seeing Piper again after all these years and coming up with a myriad of scenarios of what could happen. In some daydreams, tears were shed as we hugged each other, and in others we ended up throwing our drinks in each other's faces. My mind whirled, dancing from one extreme to the next, preventing me from falling back to sleep.

I also couldn't get Andy out of my head. My brain kept coming up with the most ridiculous ideas. I'd come up with reasons why it would never work, to get my mind and heart to see reason. The top of that list being my sudden feelings were probably not reciprocated. Then, of course, on the off chance that they were, there was also the fact that I was leaving the day after Christmas, and I lived on the other side of the country. But then I'd find myself wistfully dreaming of throwing caution to the wind and making out with Andy by the falls. I'd then push that aside by picturing him with the redheaded police officer . . . whatever her name was. And then I wanted to punch things.

I'd stopped by Miss Anna Cate's last night after dinner at Andy's parents' house. I wanted to see how she was and talk to her, maybe get her opinion on the whole thing. She had been someone I'd confided in about this kind of stuff back in the day, and she always had the best advice. But when I got there, she was exhausted and looked worn out, and not long after she invited me in, she fell asleep on the couch. I putted around her place, too wound up to sit, cleaning up the kitchen and dusting some of the living room before covering her with a big blanket and letting myself out the door.

I really needed someone to talk to—besides Andy, obviously. It was all very frustrating. In the end, I figured out on my own that it was probably best for me to push any thoughts of Andy and romance out of my head and focus on the friendship that I had just gotten back. Why would I ever want to jeopardize that?

I really had to focus on that because Andy was coming with us today since it was his idea, and also, I figured it would be good to have a third party. Not that I really expected Piper and me to throw drinks in each other's faces, but you never knew. We might both have

PMS. I'm pretty sure I didn't, but I was never any good at keeping track of all that.

"Hey gorgeous," Andy said as I met him outside the cottage. He gave me a quick peck on the cheek. My heart started sputtering at the sight of him, and his compliment didn't help matters, causing the butterflies to start fluttering around. This was not going to work.

"I'm nervous," I admitted to him, pulling my camera strap up on my shoulder and tugging on the bottom of the form fitting cream jacket I'd painstakingly chosen to wear. I wanted to wear something completely opposite of the last time Piper saw me—which was a black tee shirt, black jeans, and Converse, since that's what I'd worn pretty much every day of high school. I wanted something bright and feminine. So cream it was. I paired it with a pale-pink flowy blouse, skinny jeans, and nude heels.

"Why are you nervous? It's Piper," he said, the corner of his lip moved upward and he squinted one eye—very pirate like.

"It's more complicated than that," I said, adding an eye roll for emphasis.

"Why?"

"Because I don't know how she's going to react. What if she throws her drink in my face?"

He tilted his head to the side—giving me the sardonic look my mom often gave me. "She's not going to throw her drink in your face."

"You never know. She might have PMS."

"What? That's ridiculous."

"Oh, never mind. You're a dude, you just don't get it.

Come on," I said, grabbing his arm and leading him in the direction of Tinsel's.

We walked the short distance to the coffee shop, made our way into the small space, and found a table in the corner. As we sat down I felt fidgety, like I needed to be doing something. I started messing with my camera, which was now sitting on the table next to me.

"Relax," Andy said, reaching over and grabbing my hand. I quickly yanked it away from him, because his touch was definitely not going to help me relax.

He gave me an odd look. I didn't want to make him feel bad for pulling away, so I set to work taking my phone out and using the camera in selfie mode to make sure I didn't have anything stuck in my teeth. This was moot because I hadn't even eaten anything yet today. I was too nervous to eat.

I heard the bells on the door ring and slipped my phone back into my purse, feeling nerves pulse through me. I looked up and there she was. Piper. My best friend for so many years of my life. I would have recognized her anywhere with that same dark brown, perfectly styled hair, that stunning beauty that had barely aged. She looked the same, but with an unmistakable maturity that only added to her beauty.

When I'd envisioned seeing her—in the version where we didn't throw our drinks in each other's faces—I had pictured her coming to the table, where we'd most likely embrace, she'd have a seat, and we would talk. All civilized-like. But when I saw her, I couldn't help myself. I practically ran to her, put my arms around her, and promptly cried. I had missed this girl so much, I didn't even know how much until I saw her walk through that door.

We probably looked like complete idiots, but I didn't care. It was just like old times—but it also wasn't. Because we were adults now and so much had happened since the last time we saw each other, but it was like none of that mattered now.

I stepped back from her, out of our hug, both of us were smiling and wiping at our eyes.

"Come on," I said, grabbing her hand and dragging her over to the table where Andy was patiently waiting.

"So, you look amazing," I said after we took a seat across from each other.

"I was going to say the same about you," Piper said, her eyes still glossy from the tears.

"Well, you know," I lifted my shoulders briefly. "The goth thing got kind of old."

She smiled. "You look like . . . you."

My stupid eyes filled with tears again. Piper still knew me. After all this time.

She took a big breath. "I'm so sorry—"

"Let's not even talk about it," I said, waving her words away with my hand.

And that was it. No yelling or throwing drinks in each other's faces. No hashing it out or talking about it until we were sick. That's all that needed to be said. If only we had done this years ago.

Then, with all of that so easily out of the way, we talked. It felt just like old times, like we fell right back into the ease of being Piper and London—just as it had been with me and Andy. She asked me about my life, and I gave her a brief version, wanting to know more about her.

She told me about being a mom, gushing about her little boy, Finn. I couldn't believe Piper was a mother. I mean, I could—she always was the more nurturing of the two of us. The way she talked about Finn and what happened with his dad made me sad that I wasn't there for her through all of that—not that I could have changed anything. But I could have been a shoulder to cry on; I could have seen her through it all.

So much time had been lost, but as we sat in the coffee shop, I didn't want to dwell on that—not right now, not when I had her back. Wanting to lighten the conversation, I asked her about some rich old guy that Andy had mentioned she was dating—someone she had met at work. She tried to tell me nothing was going on, but I knew it was more than that. I could still read that face of hers after all these years. I figured she didn't want to say too much in front of Andy, seeing as they were coworkers and all, so I asked him to go get us drinks. That was just what she needed, because once Andy left, she filled me in on all the details. It really did feel like old times.

"Are you and Andrew an item?" she asked after she was done telling me about Jace—the guy she met at the resort who apparently was not that old, but was, in fact, very rich.

Me and Andy . . . an item? I guess I wasn't the only one who could still read a face. This had me feeling like I wanted to go into a panic. Because if Piper could read me, could Andy as well? Oh gosh, I didn't want to contemplate it.

I held back the freak-out I felt coming on, and in a forced calm voice said, "What, Andy? No, we're just friends." I surprised myself with how even toned that sounded. Maybe I could pull this off—and not ruin things with all these feelings I'd been having.

"I think he'd like there to be more than that," she said with little head bob in Andy's direction.

"Oh," I scoffed. "That's ridiculous."

Dear heavens, I was trying too hard. She'd figure me out for sure. And wait, what did she say? He'd like more than that? Had he said something to her at work? Now was not the time or place for her to tell me, because Andy would be back at the table soon and I couldn't risk him hearing anything, but Piper and I were going to have to delve deeper into this, for sure.

Besides, I couldn't tell by the look on her face whether she was being serious or not. And then she had to remind me about how she used to tease me mercilessly about Andy and me getting together and that if I ever married him I'd be London Broll, which sounded like a beef dinner that my mom used to make. That did make us both laugh, and the laughter helped to ease the butterflies that had come to life in my stomach.

Andy came back to the table, bringing our drinks. We sat for a little longer, catching up as much as we could before Piper had to go to work. My stomach sank—I wanted her to stay and talk to me for hours. We had so much to catch up on, it would probably take days.

We agreed to do lunch or something else later that week, and as I watched her walk out, I knew that we were going to be okay. It was like it was with Andy—we just picked up and started again. Except there weren't all the conflicting feelings and heart palpitations with Piper like there was with Andy. Thank goodness.

After meeting up with Piper, Andy and I walked around the outskirts of town for a while, walking around our old high school that had been redone since we were there. We grabbed lunch back in town and then took a leisurely walk back toward the cottage, stopping to take pictures as we strolled. It was a beautiful day. The sky was an azure blue, the sun bright and warm enough that we didn't need our big winter coats. We passed by the community center and I stopped to snap a few shots again.

"Did you know it's closing down?" Andy asked, pointing to the old gray building. It was in dire need of a new coat of paint.

"Really? Why?" The community center had been the pillar of Christmas Falls for years. It's where they held the pageant on Christmas Day. All the activities that the center provided were vital to the city. How could they shut it down?

"They ran out of money, I guess. My mom was telling me about it the other day." He grabbed my hand after I stopped with all the pictures and threaded it through his arm so it was resting in the crook of his elbow, and I let him—repeating the mantra *we are just friends* in my head. *We are just friends. We are just friends. We are just* freaking *friends.*

"That's sad. I wonder why Miss Anna Cate didn't say anything about it the other day when I saw her?" The community center had been her baby, why wouldn't she have mentioned it?

"Maybe she didn't want to bother you with it," Andy said. "I mean, it's not like there's much you could do to help."

"True," I said, suddenly wishing there was something I could do. But there really wasn't. I had some savings, but no job—not even a prospective one. I had to go back to San Francisco and start all over again, career-wise. That thought made my stomach sink. San Francisco seemed so distant now—like another life.

"Hey, but there's a fundraiser tonight for it. It's a light show or something. My mom said there's a teacher from the high school that sets up these amazing Christmas lights," Andy said, bringing me back from thoughts of my other life. "You want to check it out?"

I contemplated it. I would assuredly run into people from high school. I had mixed feelings about it, curiosity being one of them. But then I remembered that the only people that had recognized me so far were Andy and Miss Anna Cate—and now Piper. If I went to this party, how many people—people I knew for most of my life—would know it was me? And if they did, what would they think of me, of what I had done with my life so far? My stomach sank as anxiety became the front-runner of my feelings.

"Or," Andy said, squeezing my hand, "we could donate some money later and just go back to your room and watch a movie?"

This was typical Andy. He could tell just by reading

my face that I was conflicted, and just like he did back when we were younger, he swept in with an alternative.

The corners of my lips pulled up into a big smile. "I think you might be my hero, Broll," I said. Putting off seeing everyone a little longer sounded like a much better idea.

"What do you want to watch?" Andy asked as he lay on the lone queen-size bed that took up most of the space in my small room. He shuffled off his shoes and made himself comfortable on the stacked pillows at the head of the bed.

Now that we were here, I realized I hadn't thought this through properly. When Andy offered to watch a movie with me, saving me from my addled brain, I'd jumped right on it. But now he was in my room, on my bed, all cozy-like. My heart picked up its pace and the room suddenly felt warm. Too warm. I took off my jacket and hung it in the closet. Then I took a seat on the comfortable dark green arm chair, keeping my distance from the bed. I pulled my feet up onto the chair and wrapped my arms around my knees.

Andy looked over at me and then patted the space next to him on the bed.

"What's wrong?" he asked, looking confused when I didn't make a move from the chair.

"Nothing. I just thought I'd give you more room on the bed. It's . . . uh . . . small."

"It's bigger than the bed in my room," he said, referring to his full-size bed that we were squished on at his parents' house just yesterday. "Come on," he coaxed, patting the space next to him again.

"I'm good," I said. "What do you want to watch?" I grabbed the remote from the side table that was between the bed and the chair I was sitting in, and powered on the television.

I could feel Andy staring at me, but I kept my gaze on the TV.

"What do you want to watch?" I asked again when he didn't answer.

"Walsh," he finally said, "why are you being so weird?"

I wanted to protest, I wanted to tell him that I was being normal, and it was *him* that was acting all strange. But I *was* being weird. I looked like a total fruit-loop right now, sitting in this chair. High school London would have been on that bed the second Andy lay down. The problem was, grown-up London—or not-so-grown-up, as it were—was having all the feelings at the moment, and wasn't sure how to compartmentalize all of that. I needed to do some major compartmentalizing where Andy was concerned.

"Get over here," he said.

I sighed. I was avoiding these feelings that I had been having for Andy because I didn't want to ruin things between us. And here I was, making things weird anyway.

"Okay, fine," I said, making my way to the bed.

"Took you long enough," he said as I lay down next to him.

I was rigid at first, my legs straight, my hands and arms by my side. I felt very "light as a feather, stiff as a board," like we used to play during slumber parties when I was a kid. I was near the edge of the bed, trying to keep some distance between us.

But it all felt wrong; I was making it weird again. Or rather, even more weird. So when Andy slid a hand underneath my shoulders and pulled me toward him, I let him. And that gesture—small as it was—had me melting into him. Without overthinking it, I found myself putting my head on his shoulder and wrapping my arm around his waist, shifting myself toward him until there was no space between us. We were like one body on that bed, nearly unidentifiable where I began and he ended. And it was heavenly. I snuggled into him and he smelled like soap and remnants of cologne.

"Much better," he said, reaching a hand up and gently touching my hair, pushing his fingers through the ends.

My heart—my freaking heart—was doing double time. I briefly pondered moving my head over just enough to be able to hear his heart and see if the proximity between us was having any effect on him, but I didn't. I stayed just where I was.

Ten

"ALL OF THIS HAS BEEN so hard. I can't believe you aren't here," my mother said to me over the phone the next morning.

I wanted to say that I probably wouldn't have been there anyway. I would have been back in San Francisco. And none of this was really my problem, since we were all adults and the divorce was her and my father's decision. But she seemed distraught, and I didn't want to add to it . . . or get lectured for it.

"I know, Mom," I said for like the fiftieth time. I would have agreed that I should have been there, but that would have been a lie. I was convinced that Christmas Falls was exactly where I should be, and the thought of leaving here felt so wrong. I was starting to feel over-whelmingly sad over the fact that I was going to have to leave here soon enough as it was.

"You should come home early. I can't believe you'll be away from us for Christmas."

"But I'll be home the day after Christmas and I'll stay for New Years, remember?" I wished she didn't remember, because I was regretting that. Why had I offered to do that? I know it was to appease her at the time, but now the thought of being there—my home that hadn't ever felt like home—for a whole week depressed me. The assuredly odd dynamic that would blanket the atmosphere as we tried to navigate our way through the new family my parents were creating by divorcing. I didn't want to say broken, even though that's what was happening. It felt too sad.

"Savannah and Boston aren't around much either," she said, her voice sounding tired and morose. Guilt worked its way up my spine, like a slow-moving spider. But I pushed it away because this wasn't on my shoulders. Savannah and Boston could step up as well. Why did this stuff always fall on me, anyway?

"Sorry, Mom. In just over a week, we'll all be together."

"True," she said.

"How's Dad?" I asked tentatively, not sure what she'd say about him. She'd never vented her feelings about my dad to me, probably wanting to keep the kids out of it, but I imagined at some point she would start.

"He's right here. You want to talk to him?"

Huh? "Dad's there with you?"

"Well, yes, of course. Where else would he be?" I knew she was giving me the what's-wrong-with-you head tilt right now, even though I couldn't see her.

"Uh, because you're getting divorced?"

"Well, yes, but where else would he go?"

"I don't know—I don't have any experience in this area—but wouldn't he go to a hotel or find an apartment or something?"

"And waste all that money? No," she said. "He's just sleeping in the guest room right now until we sort things out."

Oh my gosh, my parents were so weird. Seriously, who does that? What kind of divorce was this? And why didn't they just stay married but have different rooms? So many people did that when they got older.

I sighed. "Just tell Dad hi for me. I've got to go," I said, ready to get off this call and go back to pretending that my parents weren't having this ridiculously civilized divorce. It made it easier to accept that it was over if they didn't like each other. This whole thing was messing with my head.

To clear my thoughts after speaking with my mom, I took a drive up to Gatlinburg with my camera, ready to go check out the downtown area and hopefully find some interesting things that I could photograph and "goth up" to add to my Etsy store.

The drive from Christmas Falls to Gatlinburg was clear, with no traffic on the two-lane road as I made my way. I loved this entire drive. The mountains all around with peaks covered in snow. The evergreen trees covering most of the ground with their green, spindly needles. I loved to do this drive in the summer, especially with the window down. The smell of dirt, trees, and wildflowers all mixed together. I really did love it here.

I didn't have as many compliments for the big city of San Francisco. Sure, it was exciting and had a beauty of its own. But it was also crowded and people weren't so kind as they made their way to their destinations. Here there was an air of ease—a slow-paced existence.

I found a parking spot on the side of the road, which was unheard of this time of year. It was like a sign that I was supposed to be here today.

My phone beeped in my purse as I grabbed my stuff and got out of my car.

Andy: What are you up to?

A thrill went up my spine, and I told that thrill to shut up. I had been forcing thoughts of him out of my head all morning, trying to stop this nonsense.

Me: Just driving around.

I didn't want to tell him that I was in Gatlinburg—near his work—because my girly brain was up to no good with that. If I told him and he invited me to the resort, then I'd probably jump at the chance. And if he didn't invite me, I'd read into it forever and it would take up my brain space. There was not much space left in there. I needed a breather today. I needed to think about things. I needed to sort it all out.

Andy: Don't get lost with your gas light on.

I laughed when I saw his response. He was referring to the time in high school when we got lost driving around the Smokies. There was no cell service, and angels must have been watching out for us because the gas light was on, but we never ran out of gas. I was nervous and anxious, and despite that, Andy had me laughing the whole time. He was always able to do that.

I wrote him back.

Me: I'll try not to. It's a big world out there.

Andy: I'd miss you if you got lost.

I had to force myself to not read into that comment.

Me: You'd come find me, right?

Andy: Depends on whether there's anything good on TV tonight.

I laughed out loud at that and then slipped my phone back into my purse. A lift in my spirits just from getting a text from Andy. That was silly.

The ever-growing strip of shops in Gatlinburg were bustling with sightseers. This had always been one of my favorite towns to go to, even with the tourists. I liked to stay on the end where there were mostly cutesy stores and fewer large attractions, which seemed to cheapen the area, in my opinion. There were many shops I recognized, and some new ones interspersed throughout that had shown up over the past eight years.

I stopped to take pictures of objects that I thought could easily be manipulated. A cool looking doorknob on an old-timey photo shop, the base of an old bench that was ornate and finely detailed, a portion of a tree that was knotty and oddly shaped. There was so much of this around here; I was excited at the prospects of what I might do to manipulate these pictures into something deeper.

I wandered over to the back of a strip of buildings, wondering if the stone path that used to be there was still around. I remembered exactly where to go; I'd been there many times before. It was still there, but the surrounding area had changed so much that I almost missed it.

A couple, around my age, was being photographed by a man who looked to be in his early forties. He was directing them and telling them to gaze into each other's eyes. Engagement pictures, I would presume. The couple was attractive, but I wouldn't say model material, so this wasn't some sort of lifestyle shoot. I kept my distance, photographing fallen leaves that were still on the ground and had taken an interesting shape. I wanted to take some up-close pictures of the rocks that made up the path, but I would have to wait until the photographer was done.

It had been a long time since I'd taken pictures of people. I'd had family members that wanted me to take their pictures, but I always found some excuse to decline. I wanted to photograph people, but when I tried, I was never any good. Maybe I shouldn't have practiced by taking pictures of my niece and nephew—Savannah's kids. They moved so fast, the pictures were all blurry.

"Excuse me," I heard a man say as I was snapping a picture of a tree root that jutted out behind a mossy rock.

I turned around to find the photographer that had been taking pictures of the couple standing near me.

"Sorry," I said, thinking that I had somehow gotten in the way of his photography session.

"For what?" he asked, looking flustered and irritated.

"Did I get in your way?"

"No," he said, shaking his head back and forth. "I was wondering if you could help me."

"Uh," I said, looking around. The couple was still

standing over on the stone path, not paying attention to us.

"I would pay you," he said.

"I'm sorry . . . for what?" This guy was super awkward—from his ancient-looking belted jeans and tucked-in, wrinkled polo shirt, to his disheveled light brown hair.

He balanced his camera in one hand, holding his other hand out for me to shake, which I did, reluctantly. "I'm Don," he said.

"Nice to meet you, Don." I was still none the wiser, except now I knew his name.

"See, my assistant quit on me yesterday, and I could use a hand with this engagement shoot." He pointed over to the couple, still in the same spot, now making out.

"Uh, what would I need to do?" I wasn't even sure why I was asking. I should just tell him no and head back to . . . well, to not much. Andy had to stay late at work tonight, so I didn't have any real plans.

"Just hold the light reflector for me, maybe take some shots of your own for a different perspective," he nodded with his head at my camera.

"I don't know, I haven't taken a lot of pictures of people," I said.

"Let me see your work," he said, again motioning toward my camera with his head.

"I . . . uh . . ." I handed him my camera without really thinking it over. He could run off with it. Not that he would—my camera paled in comparison to the one he was holding in his hands. His camera was an advanced Nikon with a high-priced zoom lens that made mine look like the dinosaur of cameras. I'd always wanted a Nikon but never could afford it, especially with the paltry earnings I'd gotten from my Etsy sales.

I watched his face as he looked through the viewfinder of my camera, scanning through the pictures I had taken since I'd been here.

"I like your work," he said, handing me my camera back.

"Thanks." I put my camera strap over my shoulder.

"So, what do you say? I'll pay you two hundred to help me out," he said, the corner of his mouth lifting up into a half-smile.

"You saw my pictures," I said, looking down at the camera hanging by my waist.

"Yeah, so?" he asked.

"I'm not good at photographing people." There wasn't one picture of a human in all three hundred pictures on that camera.

"It's not much different. You're good at capturing light. Anyway, I can teach you, I've had lots of experience."

"Well—"

"I'm kind of in a bind. What do you say?" he looked like he was trying to be patient, and it was taking everything out of him to do it.

"Sure," I heard myself say, and immediately regretted it. How long would I be stuck helping this stranger?

"Great." He motioned for me to follow him over to the couple who were still gazing lovingly at each other, not even caring that their photographer had just hired a complete stranger to help him.

"This is . . . uh," he went to introduce me to the couple, but then realized he didn't even know my name.

"London," I said.

"London," he repeated. "This is Madi and Will," he said pointing to the couple. "London's going to help us out today."

He twisted a collapsed disc that opened into a large silver circular form and handed it to me. I recognized it as a light reflector, but that was about the only thing I knew about the item I held in my hands. I think he fully expected me to know how to use it because he gave me no guidance or direction after he handed it to me. I awkwardly held it in my hands, not knowing where I should go, or what I should even be doing with this thing.

"London, stand over there," he said pointing to the other side of where he was once again shooting the couple. He moved me around until I was holding it how he wanted and then he started shooting again.

We did this for a while, him moving me around until I started to see what he was going for, how he wanted the light reflected, and then I was able to figure out on my own where he needed me without him asking. He gave me a quick nod the first time I did this, acknowledging the fact that I had done it correctly, and it seemed like he might be impressed.

This went on for an hour or so, moving the couple around in the area, Don posing them and taking pictures, with me holding the light reflector when he needed it. When he didn't, I practiced taking some pictures myself, making sure I didn't distract him or the couple.

"Thanks for your help," he said as he packed up his

camera bag. The couple—Madi and Will—had walked off hand in hand a few minutes before.

I handed him the reflector and he collapsed it with ease, adding it to his bag.

"I have another client in about thirty minutes. Does that work for you?"

"Oh," I said, thinking this had been a one-time deal.

"Yeah, I should have specified back there. I need someone for the day," he said.

"Um, sure," I said, still reluctant, but also now a little curious. Assisting Don, while it hadn't been the most glorious job, was certainly an interesting one. And I learned a lot, even just standing there. Watching the way he moved the couple around, posing them the way he wanted so that they looked completely natural, rather than posed. It was fascinating.

I spent the rest of the afternoon following Don around to different locations, helping him with whatever he needed, soaking up whatever info he'd give me or that I could learn as I watched him work. I was like a sponge, taking it all in. He had clearly been doing this for a long time.

"Here you go," he said at the end of the day, handing me two hundred-dollar bills.

"Thanks," I said, taking it from him and pocketing it. "It was nice to meet you." I held out a hand and he shook it with a nice, firm grasp.

"So how about tomorrow?" He slung his overflowing camera bag over his shoulder.

"Tomorrow?"

"Yeah, I need someone for tomorrow too."

I stood there contemplating my day tomorrow. I didn't really have anything going on, except for hopefully seeing Andy—who'd be at work all day anyway. At least this would give me something to do. Plus, I'd learned so much already today. What could Don teach me tomorrow?

"Yeah, okay," I said, feeling like I was in a dream sequence or something. This was all totally strange.

"Great. I'll meet you at my studio at eight-thirty," he said, reaching into his pocket and handing me a business card with the words "Don Shields Photography" printed across the top in raised gold lettering.

I laughed to myself as Don and I went our separate ways and I headed toward my car. I'd spent a lot of time taking pictures in Gatlinburg when I lived here before and had run into my fair share of odd things. But this was definitely at the top of the list.

Eleven

THE NEXT MORNING, I MET Don at his studio, which was not much more than an office behind the main shopping area of Gatlinburg. The furniture inside was modern in gray tones and the walls were white and sparsely covered with large prints mounted on rustic wooden frames of families and beautiful scenery presumably taken by Don.

I'd Googled him last night like any normal person would, and to put it lightly, Don Shields was kind of a big deal. There were pages and pages of entries—he started working as a photographer for a large publication in Manhattan. From there he dabbled in photographing fashion models and working for some of the biggest magazines in the world. He eventually gave all that up and settled in Tennessee where he'd met his wife; they had two children. He said in one article that family and outdoor photography had always been his first passion, and he was loving being back here.

The prices he charged, though . . . oh my gosh. His starting price for one session was almost as much as I made working a full week at my last job in San Francisco. How people could afford to hire him was beyond me, but he was a coveted photographer, his website touting that he was booked through the spring already.

We spent the day with two separate families, one was visiting from somewhere north and the other was local to Gatlinburg. Both sessions went smoothly. I aided wherever I could, holding reflectors, handing him lenses, and assisting however he needed me to. I, in turn, soaked up any and all information he'd pass along, committing to memory how he did what he did. It was fascinating and fun, and I found myself wondering if someday I could be in his shoes doing the same thing. I'd never wanted to take pictures of people because I'd never really given it a fair try. Now that I'd gotten my feet wet, I'd found that it might be something I'd like to do.

I explained it all to Andy over hot chocolate and then a walk to the falls later that evening. It was still early, and I was twitching for my camera I'd left back in my room so I could capture the falls with the pinks and oranges reflecting off it as the sun set behind the Smokies.

"Sounds like you might've found your calling," Andy said after I talked his ear off about Don and everything I had learned. I wondered how he could care all that much about it, but he seemed like he did.

"Oh, and get this," I said, hitting his arm with the back of my gloved hand. We were wrapped up in winter coats, hats, and gloves. It was particularly cold that evening. "Don wants to hire me to work for him."

"Here? In Gatlinburg?"

"Yeah. Isn't that crazy? That's crazy, right?"

Don had insisted that I show him the pictures I had been intermittently taking when he didn't need my help during the shoots. He said he was impressed by my work, and then he offered me the job to be his assistant.

"What did you say?" Andy asked. We were standing side by side looking out at the falls.

"I told him I'd think about it. But really, I mean, there's no way." Even when I'd said I'd think about it, I knew there was no way I could move here. I blamed it on the fact that everything I had was in San Francisco—but really, that was a lot of change with too many variables.

Andy gave me a serious glare. "You should do it."

"What? Move here?" I shook my head. It just wouldn't work.

"Why not? I mean, you said yourself it would be like a dream job."

I had told him that in my ramblings about my day. And I hadn't been lying. These past two days of work hadn't felt like work at all. It was like the stuff I did for my Etsy store, except I actually made some money. Still, though, there were too many unknowns if I picked up and moved here. I mean, where would I even live?

"I don't think so. My life is in San Francisco for now," I said to Andy.

"Is it? You don't talk very fondly of it."

This was true. I don't think I had said one nice thing about living in San Francisco since I'd been back in Christmas Falls. That's because when I compared the two in my head . . . well, there was no comparison.

I sighed. "I mean, I don't have anything here—my family lives in Phoenix which is closer to San Francisco. I guess I have Piper now . . ."

"And me," Andy said, and I turned from the falls to see his serious face, no trace of a teasing smile on his lips.

I let out a breath. I did have Andy—and he felt like everything right now. I stepped closer to him to give him a hug, to show him how much I appreciated him. But instead, on a whim, I lifted up on the tips of my toes, and I kissed him. It was a quick kiss, a light one. It was enough, though, that it was not just a step over the friend zone boundaries, but a flying leap.

"Sorry," I said, the word rushing out of me as I stepped back and away from him. What had I just done? It was such a knee-jerk reaction, like my brain wasn't even involved. I must have been high on all the photography stuff or something. My body had worked as if on autopilot.

"It's . . . okay," he said. He looked as if I had punched him—confused, mixed with something else. I wasn't sure. Either way, it was not a good look. There was my answer, then. At least I knew how he felt now, and it wasn't some huge declaration on my part that couldn't be taken back. It was just a kiss. No big deal.

"Sorry," I repeated, thinking that I probably should turn around and walk away from him. From what I'd just done.

"What was that?" he asked, the space between his eyebrows crinkling together.

"I . . . I don't know," I said. "I just got caught up in the moment or something. Just," I closed my eyes and shook my head. "Just pretend like it didn't happen, okay?" I opened my eyes to see his expression hadn't changed. So much regret ran through me right then.

"Why, though?"

I felt moisture start to fill my bottom lids, ready to spill over. What a dumb thing to do. And the look on his face . . . oh, if I could just go back and stick to the hug that I had originally meant to do.

"I don't know. I just kind of wanted to do it . . . to kiss you. I've been having all these weird feelings since I've been back, and then there was Mrs. Mitchem, and this weird dream," I was rambling and I couldn't stop myself. "And I know it's probably not the same for you, but I can't stop thinking about you—and not in a friendly way. In a stupid girly way." So much for not making any declarations that couldn't be taken back. I'd really messed this up.

"London—"

"I know," I said cutting him off with my words and holding a hand up as well. "I know, we're friends. It would be stupid to ruin that, and I probably *did* just ruin it. And I'm really sorry, I'm . . . I'm just really sor—"

My last word was cut off by Andy—by his lips. His arms were around me and he was kissing me. His lips were on mine, moving so intensely almost . . . almost like they were making up for years of pent-up passion. And it took me only a second to recover from the shock of it. Then I was returning his kiss, my arms wrapping around his waist and pulling myself into him like I couldn't get close enough. His mouth coaxed my lips to part, for my mouth to open so he could deepen the kiss. I followed his lead, returning the kiss with as much fervor and intensity as I could.

It was . . . perfect. My heart was beating in my chest and my stomach was swirling with that delicious feeling of butterflies that happens when everything feels right. And it did feel right, almost too right. Warmth spread through me from head to toe, and I felt weak and strong at the same time. This was so much better than the kisses my pathetic girly brain had conjured up over the past few days.

We kissed for a while like this, like we were making up for lost time. Then the movements of our lips started taking on a slower pace, less frenzied and lust filled, moving into something more tender and gentle. When Andy finally pulled his mouth away and rested his forehead on mine, we were both breathless, and I felt lightheaded, almost drunk on all the feelings that were rushing through me.

I kept my eyes closed. I didn't want to open them; I didn't want this to end. I didn't know what would come next, and that frightened me because I knew things would be different between us now, and it would be hard to go back. I didn't want to go back.

My arms still wrapped around him, I could suddenly feel Andy's body trembling. I looked up to find him doing that thing where you're trying so hard to hold in laughter that your body is shaking from it.

"Are you laughing?" I felt something like mortification move quickly through me. Had this been a joke?

"Oh my gosh," he said, now letting it out as his laughter became audible.

"Why are you laughing?"

"London," he said, trying to pull himself together. "That was . . . I just . . . Oh, my gosh."

"Spit it out, Broll," I said, feeling annoyed and trying to get away from him, but his arms were tight around me and he wasn't going to let me go.

His laughs turned to chuckles and then he stopped, pulling me into him and burying his head in the spot where my neck met my shoulder. He reached up and tugged down the collar of my coat and started kissing up my neck and over the bottom of my jaw until he was close to my lips.

"You have," he kissed the side of my mouth, "no idea," he kissed the other side of my mouth, "how much I've wanted to do that." He kissed me gently on the lips just once, then rested his forehead against mine.

I breathed out a sigh of relief. "Really?"

He looked me in the eyes. "Yes, really." He leaned in and kissed me gently, our mouths moving together slowly.

"Wait," I said, stopping the kiss just as he was starting to pick up the pace again. "How long?"

"How long?" He brought a hand to his chin, his look contemplative as he rubbed the base of it. "Eighth grade—that time we snuck out early in the morning and watched the eclipse."

"What?"

"Yeah," he said. "I've wanted to kiss you since the eighth grade."

"Oh, no," I said, closing my eyes and shaking my head back and forth.

"Oh . . . no?"

I sighed, opening my eyes. "We're such a cliché."

"Why?" He looked confused.

"Why? You pining for me since the eighth grade, me not knowing until we were older . . . That's like textbook cliché."

"Okay," he said flatly, angling his head to the side. "I didn't pine for you forever. I gave up around the summer before tenth grade when I realized we were never going to be more than friends. So then I pined over that redheaded girl—Carol Bellinger."

I gave him my best frown. "You totally ruined the story."

"But you just said we were a cliché," he squinted his eyes at me.

"Yeah, but I liked the cliché," I pouted.

"If it helps, I always held a small candle for you."

"That helps a little." I added in a sniffle for good measure.

"So," he said, a soft smile on his lips.

"So," I echoed.

"What do we do now?"

"Well, I don't know about you, but I'd like to kiss you some more," I said.

"That sounds like a solid plan," he agreed, pulling me to him and claiming my lips with his.

Twelve

I WAS, IN A WORD, high. High on life, high on Christmas, high on all the girly feelings, and definitely high on sugar cookies. I had gone to the bakery this morning and grabbed some more.

Last night was . . . well, magical. That's the only word to describe it. Andy and I made out by the falls for a while and then came back to my room at the cottage and made out some more. It was like being a teenager again. I kept wondering, what if we had done this in high school? So many wasted years. But then again, maybe Andy and I weren't ready for each other back then. Maybe it had to happen now because we needed all that life experience between us before we could be together.

And I was getting ahead of myself. We kissed. A lot. But there were no declarations of anything. No promises of a possible future. I lived across the country, for crap's sake. But I had to admit to myself, in all the dates and boyfriends and kisses I'd ever had, it never felt like this. It was almost too easy. Andy had been one of my best friends, and even though we had drifted apart, when I got here and we ran into each other, we just picked right up.

It *was* almost too easy. Like it was meant to be. And if I thought too hard on that, it scared me to my core. So I didn't think about it. I pushed it away and enjoyed the newness of it all. Whatever *it* was.

Don had only one client in the mid-afternoon, and I went into Gatlinburg to help him. If nothing came of working for him, at least I could help pay for this trip, as my savings were slowly starting to deplete. And also, the wealth of knowledge just from the past three days was worth it. The thought of moving here and working for him played on repeat in my head while I assisted him with the shoot. Of course, those thoughts were intermixed with flashbacks of Andy—kissing him, holding him . . .

I couldn't believe I was actually entertaining thoughts of moving here. Going back and forth about the pros and the cons. But I had to admit the "pro" column was slowly gaining check marks. I could be here, back in Christmas Falls, back in the only place I ever felt at home. I could start over. I had a job offer. I could be near Andy . . . and Piper. Who knows what other friendships I could build. I could be here for Miss Anna Cate.

Some of those same things were in the "con" column as well. What if being back here suddenly didn't feel like home? And starting over was hard. There were many logistics and stumbling blocks—like paying to move, getting out of my apartment lease, finding a place to live here. What if things didn't work out with Andy, and I was stuck in this small town where everyone knew everything? I'd never get away from it. What if Piper moved away? And I'd be here to watch Miss Anna Cate die. I didn't know if my heart could handle that.

After I finished up working with Don, I walked around Gatlinburg, taking pictures with my camera—this time I had people in some of them. Not faces, but I snapped a picture of an old man's hand holding a cup of coffee, and the feet of a boy sitting on a bench with his shoelaces untied. I wasn't sure I could add these to my online store because I had no idea how they'd turn out. But it was exciting to try something different.

I went back to my room at the cottage in the early evening, wanting to call Andy, but not having a reason to, except that I wanted him to come over so we could have a repeat of last night. We'd texted a few times during the day, just a few quick texts to say hello and acknowledge the fact that we were both thinking about each other. It was also annoying that I felt like I needed a reason to call him—if this had been a couple of days ago I would have just sent him a text demanding that he come entertain me. But now? Now it felt every move I made meant more.

After about thirty minutes of debating whether to call Andy or not, there was a light knock on my door, and I ran to answer it. I didn't even bother asking who it was before I opened the door.

Before I could even properly greet him, Andy's arms were around me, his lips were on mine, and he was slowly moving into the room. With a smooth move, he shut the door behind him as he guided us farther into the room without breaking the kiss.

"Hi," he said after we came up for air. He had a hand wrapped around my back holding me close to him, his other palm was on my cheek, fingers pushing into my hair.

"Well, hello," I said, feeling breathless and light and happy—oh, so very happy. I couldn't remember the last time I'd felt this way, this feeling of elation that moved through my entire body, from the top of my head down to the tips of my toes.

He grabbed my hand and walked me to the dark green armchair where I had awkwardly curled up the other night to keep my distance from him. There would be no awkward distance between us tonight, apparently. He took a seat in it and pulled me onto his lap, wrapping his arms around me and holding me close to him.

"How was your day?" he asked me, pressing light kisses to my neck, my collarbone, my jaw.

"It was good," I said, sounding more breathless than I meant to. "You?"

"Terrible," he said.

"Really?" I pushed back from him to get a better view of his face.

His mouth spread into a big smile. "I would've rather been with you."

"Oh," I smiled back. This Andy—this version of him—was so new to me. We'd always been able to say things to each other before, but this was on a whole other level. I liked it. It was like I had found a whole other side of him that I knew nothing about.

"You know, I think I like this side of you," I said, leaning in and giving him a soft peck on the lips.

"What side of me?"

"Well, your lips, obviously," I kissed him quickly again. "But also, this whole flirty side."

"You like?" he asked, his smile bright.

"I like. A lot."

After kissing and teasing, and I believe there was some tickling involved, my stomach made a rather loud grumbling noise. I had only eaten a couple of sugar cookies and a protein bar all day.

"Hungry?" he asked.

I looked down at my stomach. "Apparently."

"Listen, this might sound weird, so don't take it the wrong way."

"Okay." I pulled my eyebrows together.

"I don't want to go out with you tonight."

"Huh?" I might have taken it the wrong way, except this was Andy, and his grin was so wide I knew it couldn't be bad.

"Nope. I want to stay right here and have you all to myself."

There wasn't anything else I would've liked better.

We snuggled up together on the bed, our tummies full after getting takeout from the diner, watching TV, and just feeling all around good. At least I was. By the intermittent kisses from Andy, I think it was safe to assume that he was feeling the same way.

"So," he said, turning the volume down on the show we were sort of watching.

"So," I echoed.

He let out a breath. "Have you thought more about taking that job . . . about moving here?"

I let out a breath as well. I had thought about it. I'd thought about it all day. "I have," I said simply.

"And? Don't leave me hanging here, Walsh," he said, moving his chin toward his chest as he gave me questioning eyes.

"I don't know." It came out as sort of a whine.

"I knew you'd say that," he said. Reaching into his back pocket, he pulled out a folded-up piece of paper.

"You did?" I really needed to work on having an air of mystery—but I doubted that was possible around Andy.

"Yes." He unfolded the piece of paper and held it out in front of him. "Which is why I have prepared a list."

I chuckled. "A list, you say?"

"Yes, a list of reasons why London Walsh should stay in Christmas Falls."

"Don't keep me waiting, let's hear this list."

He cleared his throat. "Okay—and these are in no certain order."

"Just read it."

"Okay. Fine. Geez, you're demanding. Number one: there are four seasons here."

"What? Why is that even on the list?"

"Hear me out," he said, putting up his hand to stop my further protest. "I looked it up because I've never been there, but San Francisco doesn't have four seasons. It

125

doesn't even snow there." He said the last part like this was the most ridiculous thing he'd ever heard. "I mean, autumn is amazing here, as I'm sure you remember. And the spring is equally beautiful but for different reasons. Then there's the summer."

"I'm well aware of all that," I said, half-laughing. "But okay, I'll give you that one. The Falls has four seasons. I think it might take more than that."

"Yes, I know. Which is why that's not the only reason on my list."

"Your smarter than you look," I said, which got me a light pinch on my side that tickled and made me squirm.

"Are you going to let me finish?" he asked.

"By all means."

"Number two is that you now have a job, and you don't have a job in San Fran."

I nodded. "This is true."

"And it's a job that you might love and could catapult you to doing something you might actually enjoy. That's not on the list, I was just going off the cuff."

This guy . . . oh, man. How can you feel even more for someone you were already feeling so much for, until it seems like you're going to explode? Because that was how I was feeling.

"Number three on the list? Piper. You have Piper back now, and she needs you and you need her."

I swallowed. This was true. I did need Piper. I wanted to be a permanent fixture in her life, and her to be in mine. I hadn't had a friend like her since things went wrong, and now I wondered if those friendships only came around once in a lifetime. Maybe it was just luck that we'd found each other in the first place. And now I had her back.

"Yes, that's definitely a good reason."

"And then there's number four." He put the paper down and turned his body toward me. "Me."

My heart took off, galloping so wildly I thought it might burst out of my chest. The look in his eyes, the earnestness of his voice. I closed my eyes to try to ground myself because right then—in that very moment—I wanted to declare out loud that I wanted to stay with him forever and marry him and live in a craftsman style home where we'd fill it with a bunch of babies. Luckily, I held myself back.

"Andy—"

"I know," he said with a quick dip of his chin. He reached over and grabbed my hand, weaving his fingers through mine. "I know that it's all new and we haven't even talked about whatever this is, but it's not like we've just met. It's not like we were strangers when you showed up last week."

"I know," I said, leaning my head on his shoulder. "I just . . . I just don't want to ruin anything, you know? What if I move out here and it doesn't work out? I mean, whatever *this* is . . ."

"I think this," he said, leaning his head on mine, "is the start of something good. Something real."

I sighed contentedly. "I think so too."

Thirteen

ANDY LEFT IN THE WEE hours of the morning, and I only felt a little bad that he would be exhausted for work that day. It was, by all definitions, the best night. At least by all my definitions.

My phone rang not long after I had dragged myself out of bed. I was supposed to meet Don in a couple of hours for some afternoon and evening family shoots, and he also wanted me to give him an answer about working for him on a permanent basis. He wasn't giving me much time, which stressed me out. Even so, I couldn't help but lean toward taking it. It was just too easy—a lot like Andy and me. As if all the stars were aligning right now. As if this was all meant to be.

I picked up my phone to see who it was, hoping it was Andy. No such luck—it was my mom. After pleasantries, she dug right in.

"Can you come home a day earlier? Your father and I will pay for the ticket change fee."

"Mom," I chided. "I can't, remember? I have to sing in the pageant, and it's on Christmas Day."

"I know that," she snapped. "But couldn't you miss it? Surely you've had enough time to see everyone. It just doesn't feel right that you won't be here. None of you have ever missed Christmas with us."

This was true; it was like some unmentioned rule that we all had Christmas together. Even Savannah made sure her family was always there—giving her husband's family time on Christmas Eve. This would be the first time we weren't all together. That made my heart sink a bit. I didn't want to be the one to break tradition, and there was so much changing at home with my parents divorcing. Would this be our last Christmas all together? Would everything be different next year? I didn't want to think about that now. I was in Christmas Falls, and Miss Anna Cate needed me here. And she wasn't going to be around much longer.

"I'm sorry, Mom," was all I said.

She let out a breath. "Fine. We'll at least wait until the next day to eat the cheesecake with you." This was a Walsh family tradition. Cheesecake on Christmas. I was grateful we'd at least have that.

"So, Mom." I said this nervously, because I was feeling all kinds of apprehension.

"What is it?"

"Well, I sort of was offered a job here . . . in Gatlinburg." I wanted to make sure she knew it was in Gatlinburg and not Christmas Falls. I thought it might sit better if she knew it wasn't in the town she spent the bulk of my life trying to get out of.

"So?"

"So, I kind of want to do it."

"But you have a job. In San Francisco."

"Actually . . ."

"Oh, London." She breathed heavy into the phone. I could envision steam coming out of her ear. "Another one?"

"Yes, but I had to this time. They made Braydon my boss," I said, having full confidence this would make her realize that I couldn't work there.

"So what?"

"So what? Don't you think that would have been bad? I mean, things didn't exactly end well between us."

"I told you when you started dating that boy that you should never date someone at work," she said, giving me the reprimanding voice she was so good at.

"Yes, and I should have listened to you."

She tsked loudly. "How could you know that things would have been bad if you stayed? Can you call and get your job back?"

"Well, I don't know for sure that things would have turned out bad with Braydon as my boss, but I have a pretty good guess. And I highly doubt I can get my job back. I walked out, I didn't even give them notice." I cringed at myself when I said that. It was pretty awful of me to not at least give them two weeks. But it all had happened so suddenly. I wasn't thinking.

"And now you think you can just pick up and move across the country to Christmas Falls?" She practically spat out the words, completely forgetting that I said Gatlinburg. Obviously, she was not buying my ruse. Even though that was the truth—the job was in Gatlinburg—she knew it was Christmas Falls that was really calling to me.

"Well . . . yeah," I said.

She scoffed. "You know, you *always* do this, London."

"What do you mean?" I felt suddenly defensive. What did I *always* do?

"When things go wrong, or don't go well for you, you leave. You run."

"That's not true," I practically spat.

She laughed a sort of wicked sounding laugh. It was almost a cackle. "Oh, yes, it is. Do you know that Savannah calls it 'pulling a London' when people run away from things? Like the other day, she asked Phoenix to empty the dishwasher and Savannah said she 'pulled a London' and ran off."

I had no words. I kept trying to say something but I just kept sputtering. *Pulling a London?* Was she serious?

"Hello? London? Are you there?"

"I do not run away from things," I said when I finally got a hold of my tongue and could form words.

"You do. I'm sorry, London, but you've been that way for a long time. Any time anything hard happens, you run away from it instead of facing it. I mean, look at you right now—you're in Christmas Falls, and why?"

"Because of Miss Anna Cate," I said determinedly.

"Are you sure you didn't use Miss Anna Cate as a reason to avoid the fact that you just quit your job? Or to get away from your father and me?"

"No, I didn't." I was emphatic in my tone, but my mind . . . not so much. Tendrils of doubt started to creep in.

Had I used Miss Anna Cate and her letter to get away from my family? If my mother had called me and never mentioned getting a divorce, would I be sitting here right now, in a room at Poinsettia Cottage? I wasn't sure, but I was leaning toward probably not. I started to feel queasy. Had I used Miss Anna Cate to run away from my problems?

"Just . . . just come home, would you please?" She sounded defeated and sad.

We hung up and I collapsed on the bed. I wanted to deny it all, to call my mom back and tell her she was wrong and then send the meanest possible text to my sister since we never talked on the phone. *Pulling a London* . . . how ridiculous. But as I lay there, memories kept popping into my head.

The whole goth thing in junior high and high school . . . normally people who do the goth thing want to be part of something, to feel like they belong to a group. Not me. I had Piper and Andy and that's all I needed. So why, then? Was it to be different? Maybe. Or was it to run away from the fact that I was never going to be like my sister, Savannah, whom my mom adored. I was never going to be girly and wear pink dresses to prom. I didn't even go to the prom. When I dyed my hair black and put on all that eye liner . . . my mom, she sort of gave up on me. She didn't bother pestering me about my clothes, my hair, anything. It was so much easier that way.

And then there was what happened with Piper. I

know I ran that time. And I left this whole life behind—this life in Christmas Falls—the only place that ever felt like home. It was just easier to leave and start a new life because then I didn't have to face it all. Then there was work—five jobs since college. All of which I left on my own accord, and all because things got hard, or something changed that I didn't think I could handle. I could go on and on.

Now I was in Christmas Falls. And there was the job, and there was Andy. Oh gosh, Andy. Had he only been a pawn in all this? Did I really like him, or was he a means to help me run away from my life in San Francisco? A distraction?

As I lay on the bed, other things kept coming to mind, other times in my life where I ran away instead of facing it. My mom . . . she was right. My sister—even though I hated her for it—was right. Even right now as this all dawned on me, as I realized so much about myself, the thought that kept going through my head was: where can I go to get away from all this?

Despite wanting to do the contrary after talking to my mom, I still went to help Don with his photo shoots. Though today as I followed him around, assisting him with his shoots, my heart wasn't in it. So when he asked me if I wanted the job, I turned him down. He was disappointed and so was I, but it was the right thing to do. I needed to go back to San Francisco and work out my life there. My life was already there, I had a place to live, and it wouldn't be that hard to find a job with all the start-ups that were constantly popping up near the city. This time, though, I would find a job and I would see it through. I was determined to break this cycle. However I could.

A knock on my door had me getting up from my bed. A quick glance at the clock on the side table said it was 7:30 PM.

I knew who was on the other side of the door; I didn't even need to ask.

"Hey, gorg—" Andy cut himself off as he took in my bloodshot, puffy eyes, and my red nose. I'd been able to keep it together when I worked for Don, but since I'd been back I'd been crying about everything. My choices. The job. My mom. Andy.

"Hey, what's wrong?" he asked as I opened the door wide so he could come in.

"Rough day," I said, adding a hiccup for good measure. I was such a wreck.

"Tell me what's going on," he said, taking his jacket off and, after placing it on the chair, took a seat at the end of the bed. He patted the spot next to him and I sat.

He reached up and ran fingers along my forehead, tenderly moving to the side of my face and tucking some hair behind my ear.

"Are you okay?" he asked, searching my face. "Something happen at work?"

"No, nothing like that," I said, looking away from him and down at the tissue I was twisting around in my hands. He'd called it work, like it was my job already. But it wasn't and it never would be. I felt a lump in my throat.

"Then what?"

"It was," I started, and not being able to prevent it, moisture gathered at the corners of my eyes and large tears fell down my face. "I had a conversation with my mom."

"What did she say?"

Andy's face was so sincere as he waited for me to explain. Which made it even harder to get the words out. What was he going to think of me? But I took a deep breath and I told him. I told him what my mom said, the joke my sister had been making at my expense, and then some of the things that I had done that proved them right.

When I was done, I wanted him to put his arms around me, tell me it wasn't true, but he didn't. He just sat there.

"Oh," was all he said.

"Yeah." My brain and my heart ached so much right then. I was drained. I wanted to curl up into a ball and sleep, but wouldn't that be running away too? Or at least avoiding?

"So," Andy said, stopping himself and swallowing hard. "This whole trip—it was a way to get away from your family and from your life in San Francisco?"

"I guess," I said, wishing so badly that it wasn't true, but the feelings of guilt and remorse moved through me, and I knew that it was.

"And this," he said, motioning between us with his index finger, "was this whole thing between you and me just some means of escape for you, too?"

I wanted to scream *no* and tell him that wasn't true, that he was never a means of escape for me—not now and not before. I had never felt for anyone else the way I felt about him. And that was the truth. But I also felt raw and so conflicted. What if what I felt really was me trying to run away? What if it wasn't real?

"I . . . don't know. I . . . don't think so?"

"You . . . don't think so," he said, drawing out the words.

I just looked at him. Willing him to tell me that of course this thing between us couldn't be an escape, and to give me a bunch of reasons why. Good reasons. Real, tangible reasons. He was always good at that—talking me down, making me feel better about things.

But he didn't. And when his eyes moved to mine, the hurt that was there . . . I would never be able to scrub that picture from my brain as long as I lived. I was confident it would be stuck there forever.

"I see," he said. His gaze held steady on the floor.

"Andy," I started, but then I stopped myself. What could I possibly say right now?

"Okay, well," he placed his hands on the tops of his legs and anchored himself to stand up. "I guess it was better that I found out now rather than later."

Like later when things got bad and I ran away from it all. He didn't say it, but he didn't have to.

He grabbed his coat and left my room, not saying another word.

Fourteen

ANDY DIDN'T CALL THE NEXT morning. I didn't expect him to. My girly heart had hoped, though. I had cried most of the night, and throughout the morning I was tearing up intermittently any time I thought of the phone call with my mom, the job with Don, my life back in San Francisco . . . but the big tears happened when I thought about Andy.

After really thinking it over, I knew he wasn't a pawn in all this. He couldn't be. I truly and genuinely had feelings for him. Maybe even big feelings . . . the kind that were too early to admit out loud or even be thinking. But I also didn't trust myself right now. What if things changed, what if something went wrong and I "pulled a London"? I still had murderous feelings toward my sister over that. Maybe not murderous, but the throat-punching kind, for sure.

I had to figure out a way to get my puffy eyes to go

down and cover up the redness around my nose before I met up with Piper. She'd called me that morning to ask if I wanted to come and have dessert with her later at Blackstone Resort where she worked. I felt a little jolt at the thought that I might run into Andy there. But it was after his work hours so I doubted I'd see him.

Before that though, I had to go see Miss Anna Cate. I just knew in my heart she was the best person to talk to about all of this. Or at least I hoped she was. I knew I could talk to Piper, but she had drama of her own going on with that rich guy she'd had a thing with. Apparently that was over. I was sad for her but felt a jolt of happiness that she wanted to talk to me about it. If nothing came of this whole trip, having Piper back in my life was worth all of it. Well, mostly all of it.

I walked from the cottage over to Miss Anna Cate's house, my feet dragging. I felt heavy—in my heart, and overall. Not even the Christmas spirit of this little town could make me feel better. Although I could feel some tugging at my heart as I passed by the downtown area. I truly did love this place. It was going to be hard to leave.

"Well hello, London," Miss Anna Cate said as I stood in her doorway. She was wearing pajamas covered by a soft pink robe. "It's lovely to see you."

"Hi, Miss Anna Cate." I gave her what I'm sure was an incredibly weak smile.

"Do come in," she said, opening the door wide. I stepped through, noticing that her home looked a little different today. It felt brighter and looked cleaner than the last time I was here. Less clutter. And she even looked like she had some color back in her cheeks, though there was still swelling in her face and hands.

She offered me tea and I accepted, taking a seat in the same dark-gray wingback chair that I had sat in fewer than ten days ago when I first saw her. It felt like so much longer than that.

"What can I do for you?" she asked as she came in the room after a few minutes, carrying a tray of tea and cookies. I jumped up and took the tray from her, setting it on the coffee table as she took a seat on the couch across from me and pulled a throw over her lap and legs. I poured a cup of tea and handed it to her, and then filled one for myself.

"Why didn't you tell me about the community center?" I asked as I sat. It wasn't why I was here, but I had been curious. It was fresh in my mind since I'd walked past it on the way here.

"Oh," she shook her head, looking down at the tea cup and saucer in her hands. "I didn't want to burden you with it."

"But why?"

"Well," she shrugged, "is there anything you can do?" She gave me a doleful half-smile and I felt my heart fracture.

"I guess not," I said, wishing terribly that there was.

"Then I suppose it was pointless to talk about it. Why waste time on something we cannot change? Anyway, I suspect that's not the only thing you came to talk to me about."

"I just wanted to come say hi."

She cocked her head to the side. "Really? From the

look in those bloodshot eyes of yours, I'd say there was more to this visit."

I chuckled. Even without the bloodshot eyes giving me away, she would have seen right through me. She was always able to do that.

"Okay, so maybe there's more to my visit."

"Well, don't leave me wondering, dear. Tell me. Go on," she said, batting a hand in my direction.

I sat there for a minute, wondering what I should say, where to begin. It's not like she could tell me I wasn't the type of person to run from things, because it had become painfully obvious that it was the truth. I didn't need her to tell me that.

"I talked to my mom yesterday," I started, feeling tears fill my eyes. My emotions were on the surface right now; it was impossible to bury them.

"And?"

"I told her that I was thinking of moving here," I said.

"Oh," she said, a soft smile appearing on her face. "I don't want to lie and say that thought doesn't warm my heart . . . but it sounds like it didn't go well with your momma."

I chuckled quietly. "No, it didn't go over well."

"And what was her reasoning?"

"She thinks I'm doing it to run away from everything going on there. Like my parents divorcing."

She tsked. "I see. That really is too bad about your parents."

"Yeah, I mean it's kind of weird and totally civilized . . . they're even still living in the same house."

She shook her head. "Relationships are so different now. It's the strangest thing."

I wasn't sure if my parents were the best example of nowadays relationships. They were odd all around.

"Anyway, she told me that I've been running from things for most of my life, and when I thought about it . . . she was sort of right." There was no "sort of" about it. Saying it out loud sounded so harsh to my ears, though. I needed a bit of a buffer.

"So, what do you want to do about that?"

I breathed out heavily. "I'm not sure. I mean, first I need to apologize to you."

"Why's that?"

"Well, I think I may have used your letter as an excuse to come to Christmas Falls to get away from my family and from the job I'd just quit."

She batted a hand at me. "Oh sweetie, I don't care how you got here, I'm just happy you're here."

I smiled. Actually, I may have beamed. Leave it to Miss Anna Cate to so easily take away the guilt I'd been feeling over that.

"So now tell me what else has got ya down," she said, daintily picking up her teacup and taking a sip.

"I'm worried. What if I move here and something goes wrong. What would I do?"

She thought about that for a second. "Well, if what your momma's saying is true, you'd probably try to run."

"Right," I said, looking down at the cup of tea in my hands. Its warmth was doing nothing to help the cold I was feeling right now.

"But," she said, holding up a finger, "maybe you'd be

able to catch yourself next time. Maybe, the next time, you'd work through it, instead of running because now you know this about yourself."

"But how do I know I would?"

She shrugged. "How can we ever know something like that? No one can predict the future. And if they could, well, they'd be a rich man . . . or woman. And a pretty sad one, at that. Isn't the fun of life not knowing what's ahead, but just enjoying the ride?"

This made me tear up even more. Despite what she was saying, Miss Anna Cate did have an inkling of what was ahead of her, and yet she was so positive about everything. So positive about life.

"My mom thinks I need to come home," I said.

"And?"

"I suppose that's one of my problems. I don't know where home is. Home was never in Phoenix—where my parents live. And it's not in San Francisco either. I haven't felt at home . . . since I lived in Christmas Falls."

"And how do you feel about it now?"

"It still feels a lot like home."

"Well, you know what they say about home . . . it's a place your feet may leave, but your heart will always be." She winked at me, and I felt warmth spread like a blanket all around me.

Christmas Falls *was* home to me. It had always been home.

"But there are so many things to think about, so much that I'd need to do to be able to move here. Where would I even live? Maybe it's too—"

"Hard?" She cut me off, giving me a wide smile.

"Right," I said. That sounded an awful lot like an excuse to run away from Christmas Falls.

"Honey, you have to put in the work for something that's worth it."

That made me think of Andy. It was all new, I knew that. But wouldn't I regret not trying? Why would I base anything in my life on whether it would work out or not? I couldn't predict the future. And for once, I wanted to be around to see how it would pan out. Even if it didn't turn out how I wanted.

"And anyway, if needing a place to live is holding you back, well," she held up her arms, palms up toward the ceiling. "I've got plenty of room for you here."

"Miss Anna Cate—"

"Now don't you even start. I wouldn't offer if I didn't mean it."

"That . . . thank you, Miss Anna Cate." My eyes filled up again. I didn't want to ask this out loud for fear that it would take me off the path that I felt I was heading down, but I asked it anyway. "Do you think that moving back here is still me running away from something?"

"Maybe," she said with a shrug. "But maybe it's not running this time. Maybe it's starting new." She paused, looking me in the eyes. "Maybe you've been running because you couldn't find the place where your heart belonged. Maybe you just needed to come home."

Dessert with Piper was just what I needed. The resort was amazing, the food was outstanding. She brought her coworker Mia along and I felt an instant camaraderie with her. Like we could be fast friends. That's how it had been with Piper back when we first met. I wanted to ask Piper if she still had her bracelet that we made so long ago but then thought better of it. I would have to tell her what I did with mine – just tossing it away like I did.

I left the resort with a full belly and my heart a little bit lighter. I didn't mention anything to either of them about my conversation with Miss Anna Cate. Even though my heart warmed when I thought of moving here and starting new, thoughts of seeing where things went with Andy—if he even gave me a chance—I was still waffling. What could I say? I was a waffler. It was my thing.

Although I'd hoped—and maybe prayed—to run into him, Andy was nowhere to be seen. I only looked over the parking lot twice to see if I could find his car. Okay, I scanned it three times before I reprimanded myself for being so pathetic.

I'd really screwed that up, and I didn't know how I was going to fix it . . . if I'd be even able to. Before, Christmas Falls without Andy wasn't a big deal for me because I hadn't anticipated seeing him. Now it was like Christmas Falls and Andy were synonymous. I didn't want one without the other. But I also couldn't put that all on Andy. I couldn't move back here for him. I had to do this for me. I had to hope that if I did take the plunge, he'd be here as my friend, or hopefully even more than that.

One thing was for sure, I couldn't go talk to him until

I knew. Until I knew what I was going to do. I had to stop waffling and make a decision.

I wanted to go to the falls, where I used to go to think things through. But the memories of what happened last time I was there—being in Andy's arms, kissing him for the first time—haunted me. I knew that if I went there I wouldn't have a clear mind. I'd keep picturing myself in his arms . . . the spine-tingling chill that ran through me the first time our lips met . . . his breath on my neck . . . Maybe there wasn't anywhere to go without thinking about that. It had been on repeat in my brain since it happened. And then, because my brain was cruel, it would follow that up with the picture of Andy's face from last night—that look of hurt that I'd never forget. No spine-tingling chills there. Just an emptiness in the pit of my stomach, a heaviness in my heart.

Not knowing where to go and not wanting to go back to my room where other reminders of Andy were, I went to the community center and sat on the steps to the entrance. I did have memories here—good ones. Memories of Miss Anna Cate, of me and Piper spending time here, singing "Silent Night" with our Santa hats on. Andy and I had spent time here too, helping with after-school programs that Miss Anna Cate had set up. All good memories. They couldn't shut this place down—there had to be something we could do. Sadly, I had no resources. There was nothing I could do to save it.

As I sat there watching the stars twinkle over the town and the Christmas lights sparkle all around me, I felt the strongest need to try to at least do something. It would be easy for me to walk away from this, citing that I had nothing to give, but that wasn't true. I could do something. And I knew just what I'd do. It wouldn't be easy, and things might go wrong, but I was okay with that. I wasn't going to run from this.

Fifteen

MY PLAN CAME TOGETHER QUICKLY and almost seamlessly. I must have had a guardian angel, because usually these kinds of things never worked out for me. And then I'd "pull a London" when they didn't. But there would be none of that this time.

The next morning, I woke up early and drove into Gatlinburg. I had texted Don the night before, telling him I needed to talk to him and asking him to meet me at his office at nine the next morning. He replied with a simple "sure." It was almost impossible to sleep; my mind had been going over and over what I wanted to say to him and what I needed him to do. There were so many variables, but I had to at least try. Normally all the roadblocks would have had me running in the other direction, but not today. I was determined. I was also determined about some other things in my life, but all that would have to be put off until later. I needed to focus on the task at hand, and that was the community center.

When I got to Don's office a half hour early, I found him already there. He was ready to talk, so I took a deep breath and went in.

The deep breath was for naught. Don was on board from the minute I told him what I wanted to do, and what I was doing it for. I never even had to show him the picture of the community center I had taken to gain his sympathy. Apparently, Don had something similar in the town he grew up in and he had fond memories of the place.

It took some help from his wife, Caroline, and some favors pulled in on Don's part, but two hours later, we were set up and ready to go.

We had put up a backdrop of sorts, a very Christmas-y looking one, right off the main strip in Gatlinburg. There were props and trees and fake snow all around. I had made signs, printed them, and posted them everywhere. The sign said, "Get a picture by Don Shields, one day only!" He would take one picture—sent digitally—for a flat fee of twenty-five dollars, with a note that all the proceeds would go to the community center in Christmas Falls.

Really, it wouldn't be for the day—it would only be for four hours because Don had a client in the early evening. A client I would be helping him with, because part of the deal for today was that I would take the job as his assistant. Well, I made it seem like part of the deal; I was prepared to beg him to take me back, if necessary.

No one showed up for the first twenty minutes, and I was beginning to think that maybe nothing would come of it. I had to be okay with at least trying and not running from the idea. But not long after that, people started showing up, and then word spread until we had a line so long, I wondered if we would ever get through them all by the time we had to go to the family photo shoot later that day.

Somehow, we got through them and made it to the shoot in time. I counted the money up as Don drove us to the location for the shoot. It wasn't going to save the community center, but it was a nice chunk of change, especially for a day's work and something that had been pulled together last minute. Don also contributed some money even though I protested—he had donated his time, which meant more than he could know—but he was insistent. I took all the money I had made working for Don and added that was well.

I couldn't wait to take it to Miss Anna Cate, so after the shoot I raced back to Christmas Falls and went straight to her house.

"Here," I said as I handed her the envelope of money after she let me into her home.

Looking confused, her brows knitting together, she asked, "What's this all about?"

"This is for you." I took a deep breath—it felt like I hadn't taken a good one all day. I was surviving on adrenaline and caffeine since I'd gotten so little sleep the night before.

She took the envelope out of my hands and opened it, gasping when she saw the contents.

"It's for the community center," I said, feeling tears prick behind my eyes when I saw her look of astonishment.

"How did . . . where . . ."

I sat her down and explained the whole thing. How I asked Don to help me, and how I even found him in the first place.

"Well, this is just wonderful," she said, shaking the envelope at me.

"There's something else, though," I said, hoping she hadn't changed her mind since yesterday.

"Go on," she said with a look that said she was expecting what was coming.

"He offered me a job, and . . . I took it. And so now I was wondering—"

"If you can live here?"

"Just temporarily, until I find a place of my own," I said.

"Honey, you can stay as long as you like. As long as you can handle this old gal puttering around the house." She gave me a wink.

"I think I'd love to be here, to help you however I can," I said, and I meant it. The fear that someday I'd have to say goodbye—possibly soon—to Miss Anna Cate was still there, and there were still moments that I felt that tug . . . the tug to run. But I knew that I couldn't miss out on what time I had left with her, however long that was. I didn't know what the future held, but I wanted to find out.

I didn't stay long because there was something else I had to do. There was someone else I needed to talk to.

I pulled up near Andy's family's home and sat in my rental car a few doors down trying to work up the courage to knock on the door. My stomach was swirling with butterflies—it was a mixture of the sickening kind and the good kind. Just imagining seeing his face and what he might say to me was doing all kinds of things to my nerves.

Finally pulling myself together, I drove the car up to the front of the house and made my way to the Broll's front door.

"Well, London, to what do we owe this pleasure?" Linda Broll asked after she opened the door and found me standing there.

"I'm looking for Andy," I said, feeling like I had lost my manners, but I couldn't do small talk. There were things that needed to be said, and I needed to find Andy to say them.

"He's not here," she said looking down at her watch. "He left a half hour ago."

"Any idea where he went?" I asked, feeling my stomach sink. This was not how I pictured all this going down. I pictured him here and us going up to his room—leaving the door open, of course—and me telling him that I'm an idiot and begging him to, at the very least, be my friend again. At the very least I needed that. But he wasn't there.

"He said he had to go into town for something," she said, giving me a little shrug. "Do you want to wait for him? I was going to make cookies if you want to help."

"That sounds fun, but I think I'll go try to find him," I said, feeling antsy. I needed to see him. I needed to see his face.

She smiled. "Okay then. Maybe you can cheer him up. He's been in quite the mood these past couple of days.

He wouldn't tell us what crawled up his butt, but something's up there, I'll tell ya."

I couldn't help but giggle and hope that his being upset had something to do with me. Because that would mean he was feeling like I was.

"I'll do what I can." But even as I said it, I wasn't sure I could do anything. I only hoped I could.

"We'll see you tomorrow, right?"

"Tomorrow?"

"Christmas Eve? Andy said you were coming over," she furrowed her brow.

"Oh, yeah . . . yes," I nodded my head. "I'll be here." I felt my stomach turn. I very well might not be coming, and would have to spend Christmas at the cottage. Or maybe Miss Anna Cate would have me.

We said our goodbyes and I hopped back in my car and went back to the Poinsettia Cottage and parked there. It would take me all of thirty seconds to drive down the main strip of Christmas Falls—my mom would often say "don't blink or you'll miss it," when referring to the town. I decided driving up and down the street would probably not work, and that it was better for me to do this on foot. I would search every store if I had to.

I started at the diner and worked my way down. Most of the stores were closed at this point, but I kept going. When I got to the end of the street—to the feed store— there was no sign of him. My heart sank. I knew I'd run into him at some point, but I wanted to see him now.

Distraught and tired—the adrenaline was dissipating quickly and the sleepless night followed by an incredibly busy day was starting to sink in—I dragged my feet down the street toward the cottage. As I got to the end, though, I decided that I would take a detour and go to the falls. I was pretty sure Andy wouldn't be there, but I could at least look. At the very least I could stare at the pretty falls for a minute and maybe find some solace in them. Screw all the memories it would assuredly give me.

It was dark and there wasn't much lighting up there except for one lone lamp, but the moon was fairly bright. As I approached, the sound of the water hitting the pool below filled me with warmth and peace that felt at odds with the rush and angst of the day.

I looked over to the bench and took a quick intake of breath. A lone figure in a winter coat, hat, scarf, and gloves sat there drinking what looked like hot chocolate. I could only see his profile, but the reflection of the moon was shining off those black-rimmed glasses.

I walked over to the bench and took a seat next to him.

"Hi," I said.

Andy kept his eyes on the falls as he returned the greeting. "Hey," he said. At least he was speaking to me.

I breathed deeply. There was so much to say.

"Andy," I started.

"Don't," he said, cutting me off. "It's . . . fine."

"It's not fine," I said, feeling tears fill my eyes. His stance . . . his face . . . how was I going to make him understand? "I have things to say to you."

He let out a breath. "Okay," he said reluctantly.

"I'm sorry," I started. It felt so contrived to say those words, but they were important and true and they needed to be said.

153

"Me too," he said.

"I think we're sorry for different reasons."

I knew his sorry was for more than just the other day. There was regret in his tone. He was sorry for all of it. A tear trickled down my cheek. I knew then that I was probably not going to be able to save whatever we'd started, but I would at the very least try to save the friendship. I would try, and try, and try. I was not giving up. My heart wanted more, but I couldn't give him up entirely.

"Listen," I said, feeling him stiffen next to me. He didn't want to hear it, but he was going to. "I know I'm not your favorite person right now. I'm not even my own favorite person." This was not entirely true. I felt horrible about Andy and everything that had happened there—but the choices I'd made that day, the decisions I'd made—I was proud of that. I had done things that were out of my comfort zone and I hadn't run from it. I hadn't "pulled a London."

He turned his face toward me. It was hard to read his eyes in the moonlight, but I imagine there wasn't much love shining there. Or even much like at this point.

I continued anyway. "But I've been thinking. And I know how it seemed, the other night at the cottage. I know how it looked. But Andy," I reached over and grabbed his hand. He didn't pull away, which helped to boost my confidence. "You were never something I was using to run away. From my life in San Fran, or my parents. The letter I got from Miss Anna Cate—that's what got me here. I didn't expect to find you here, I didn't expect to feel the things I feel for you. All that? It was real. It *is* real."

He looked back out to the falls. "How do you know? How do you know for sure?" he asked, sitting back on the bench, a little less rigid.

"Because I've never felt anything like it before."

He looked down at my hand in his; he still hadn't pulled away.

"And I don't want to run from you. I want to run *to* you. Sure, I let thoughts get in my head, worrying about all the what ifs, all the risks, but for once I want to stick around and find out."

I couldn't see his eyes. Why couldn't we have done this when there was more than just moonlight and one lamp to see by? I couldn't read his face, but I could tell there was a change in his body language. He seemed to be more relaxed and not as stiff as he was when I first sat down. Maybe I was getting through to him.

"Wait," he said, his face turning toward mine. "Did you just say you're sticking around?"

I smiled, nodding slowly. "I took the job with Don. And Miss Anna Cate offered me a room at her place. And Andy," I squeezed his hand, "I don't want you to feel any pressure, we can take this slow—whatever this is—or we can just be friends or we ca—"

I was cut off once again by Andy's lips. They were on mine so fast, so intensely, I knew right then that he wanted so much more than friendship. My heart soared, because if friendship had been the only thing offered, I'd have taken it. But I wanted so much more.

"You're moving here?" he asked after kissing me soundly. His voice had a disbelieving awe to it. Like he wasn't sure it was real. I was wrapped in his arms and he was holding me tight like he didn't want to let me go.

"I am," I said. "I take it the friendship thing is off the table."

He laughed lightly. "It's *so* off the table." He pulled me in for a kiss and I chuckled against his lips.

I looked up at him. "Any chance you could take some time off to drive a girl across the country?"

"Hmm," he rubbed his jaw with his fingers. "I think I probably have to, right?"

"How's that?"

"How else am I going to ensure that you don't make a run for it instead?"

I twisted my lips at him, giving him my best pout.

"Too soon?" he asked, his eyebrows raising as he gave me a mischievous grin.

"I don't think you have to worry about that."

"I don't?"

I leaned in and kissed him softly, tenderly. "Nope. I think this time I'm here to stay."

Sixteen

THE NEXT DAY WAS CHRISTMAS Eve, and I slept in until eleven. I was so exhausted from the lack of sleep the past few nights, and staying up late last night didn't help. Andy had come back to my room after the falls, and we kissed, and talked, and snuggled, and made plans until the wee hours of the morning. It was the best night. There had been so many best nights with Andy, and I suspected there were many more to come.

I woke up to a text from Andy, who had left early this morning so I could get some sleep. And, since he was living at home, he didn't want to freak out his parents by not coming home. Heaven knows his mom would have thrown a fit.

Andy: Good morning, gorgeous.

I actually made a squealing sound—one that I'm pretty sure had never come out of my mouth—but I was so excited to hear from him even if it had only been a handful of hours since I'd last seen him.

157

Me: Merry Christmas Eve.

I had to get up because there was a lot to do before going over to the Brolls' to join their Christmas Eve celebration that night. Andy's brother, Nick, who had just gotten back into town the day before, was going to be there, and I was looking forward to seeing him. I'd get to be with the whole Broll family, like old times.

The Brolls opened presents on Christmas Eve, and it was still their tradition after all these years. I remembered being so jealous that we had to wait until the next day to open ours. Andy and I would lean out our windows Christmas Eve night and he'd show me what he got. Now I got to be part of that.

Before I could go to the Brolls', though, I needed to buy Andy a Christmas present and find something to bring as a hostess gift for his mom. I hopped out of bed and got ready for the day and then took off for Gatlinburg to do some shopping, stopping by the kitchen of the cottage where Mrs. Curtis had laid out some scones and fruit.

The sun was hidden behind clouds as I walked through Gatlinburg looking through the stores, hoping to find just the right thing for Andy. It was colder than normal. Usually this area didn't get these kinds of temperatures until the evening, and the air smelled like snow. I think a white Christmas would have probably been the icing on the cake for how I was feeling that day.

I decided that I was going to wait until the day after Christmas to break the news to my parents about moving here. I needed to do it in person. I wanted them to see my determination with their eyes so they had no doubt that I wasn't "pulling a London" with this decision. Or maybe they would still think it, and I had to be okay with that. I was twenty-six years old and my life was my own.

My heart felt lighter than it had in eight years. I was coming home.

"Merry Christmas," Linda said as she opened the door. I had made it to their house with only moments to spare. Snow had begun to fall, little white flecks dancing around in the air, just as I arrived at the porch. It was a sight to behold. I hadn't seen snow in so long.

"I brought the snow with me," I said as she opened the door wider for me to come in. She gasped when she looked out.

"IT'S SNOWING," she yelled to everyone in the house, making my ears ring afterward.

"Merry Christmas," I said after she shut the door behind me. I handed her the arrangement of Christmas flowers I'd found in Gatlinburg. It was a combination of deep red roses, orchids, branches of blue spruce, pine cones, and plaid ribbon that matched the holiday decor in the Broll home.

"These are lovely," she said, her eyes bright as she looked them over. She took the flowers from me as I juggled a few things—a box of sugar cookies from the bakery and a couple of presents that I'd found for Andy.

I'd shopped for boyfriends before, and it was always stressful. There was always the worry that whatever I got would mean too much, but it also had to be enough that it was thoughtful. With Andy, there wasn't so much angst. I knew him. I knew what he liked, and when I found what I was looking for, I just knew. It was easy. Kind of like how it had been all along. We made sense, Andy and me. I just wished it hadn't taken me so long to figure it out.

Andy came rushing down the stairs when he realized I was there, his feet pounding on the hardwood as he made his way to me. He took the packages out of my hands and leaned in and kissed me.

"Merry Christmas," he said, and the soft way he said it, almost a whisper, had the butterflies that were already swirling in my stomach doing leaps and flips.

"Excuse me?" Linda asked after Andy had kissed me again and then turned around to face his mother.

"Oh, yeah. I suppose I should have told you before now, but London and I are a thing."

"A thing?" she questioned. She looked almost horrified.

"Yep," he said, putting the presents he had taken from me in one arm and wrapping his other arm around my waist, pulling me close to him.

She gawked at us. But then slowly, her lips curled up into a smile. "Well, I'd say this is a good thing, then." She looked back and forth between us. "Yes," she smiled. "This is good."

Andy leaned in and kissed me on the cheek. "I think you're right, Mom."

"NICK, BART!" Linda yelled as she carried the flowers into the kitchen, placing them in the center of the perfectly set table. "ANDY AND LONDON ARE A THING NOW, OKAY?"

We both laughed as we followed behind her—my laugh was mostly out of mortification. We heard a "sounds good" from Bart, and a "'bout time" from Nick. They were both sitting in the family room watching football. The Christmas tree was all lit up and presents were overflowing underneath it. Andy walked over and set the presents I had brought him to the side of the tree, which was about the only place to put them.

Nick got up from his chair and gave me a quick hug. He looked good—no longer the punk kid that used to bother Andy and me when we were younger.

We ate dinner and then opened presents. Andy loved the gray V-neck sweater I'd gotten him and he laughed at the lizard key chain I'd found in one of the kitschy shops in Gatlinburg. He must have also been busy that day because there was a gift under the tree for me. A new camera bag for my camera.

"I love it," I said, leaning in and kissing him lightly on the lips. Linda sighed contentedly over in the corner as she caught us kissing, and I'm pretty sure my face turned all kinds of red.

After we were done, Andy grabbed me by the hand. "I have something else for you upstairs." He gave me a double eyebrow lift, and when my eyes went wide he said, "Don't worry, it's Linda approved."

"THE DOOR STAYS OPEN," Linda yelled at us as we walked up the stairs. Andy shook his head, while I laughed quietly.

We walked into his room and I took a seat on his bed.

He went over to his dresser and opened the top drawer, pulling out a thin, square white box about four inches long. It had a little red bow on the top.

"For you," he said, handing it to me.

I looked up at him as I took the small box, feeling a mixture of confusion and curiosity. What could possibly be in this box that he'd bring me upstairs to open?

I slowly slid off the lid and gasped when I saw the contents. Inside the box was my bracelet. The bracelet that Piper and I had made. The one I'd thrown away all those years ago.

"How did you . . . where did . . . ?" I couldn't even formulate a question, I was so taken aback.

"That day that you threw it after you were so mad at Piper? I went and found it." He took the seat next to me and looked at the bracelet, worn and faded from all the time I had worn it and all the time it had sat in Andy's drawer.

"I can't believe this," I said picking up the bracelet and sliding it onto my wrist. So many memories were tied to this bracelet. So many wonderful times of my life—and Andy had given it back to me.

"I figured you'd probably want it someday. I'd actually forgotten I had it until you mentioned it the other day. When I got home that night, I looked in the top drawer where I'd put it all those years ago, and there it was."

"This," I said putting a hand on his cheek, "is amazing. Thank you." I leaned in, touching my lips to his for a quick kiss, but when I started to pull away, he wrapped his arms around me and kissed me back, but the kiss he gave me was not the same quick variety that I had just given him. His kiss was much longer and passionate, and filled with so much promise of things to come.

"Welcome back, London," he whispered in my ear after we'd stopped kissing.

"It's good to be back," I said.

Seventeen

"HAVE YOU EVER HEARD OF the legend of Christmas Falls?" Andy asked as we sat on the bench in front of the falls. I was leaning into him and his arm was around me, his gloved hand rubbing slow, lazy patterns up and down my arm.

"A legend?" I asked. I vaguely remembered something, but it wasn't coming to me. That wasn't much of a surprise as Christmas night had been a bit overwhelming. Not in a bad way, more like an unbelievable fairytale way. I still couldn't fully wrap my head around it.

The people of Christmas Falls saved the community center, or at least gave it a fighting chance. It turned out I wasn't the only one who thought to donate money. Right before the pageant started, someone handed Miss Anna Cate an envelope full of donations. She was so overwhelmed, I honestly worried her heart might give out and that was going to be how her life ended. But she held strong. And she cried. I think we all did.

I didn't think the night could get any better. I might have been secretly hoping that we could just skip the pageant because nothing would top that. But I was wrong.

Before Piper and I could do a quick run-through of Silent Night, a call came in for Miss Anna Cate. A donor had been found. She was going to get a kidney. There were no guarantees, of course. But I chose to believe that it would all work out because the evening felt like it was full of magic.

Maybe the bracelets had something to do with it. Maybe they held the magic. Both Piper and I were wearing ours, both of us smiling brightly as we recognized that we still had them. I wanted so badly to tell her the tale of how I still had mine, but I would have to save that for another time.

Now I was sitting with Andy, looking at the moonlight as it fell on the falls, the stars twinkling above us. All felt right in the world, and I didn't want to leave. Except that I was beginning to not be able to feel my toes.

"Where'd you go?" Andy asked, giving me a little squeeze to bring me back to him as my mind had wondered off.

"Sorry," I said, adding a yawn for emphasis. "It's been quite the night."

He chuckled. "It has, hasn't it?"

"Okay, remind me about this legend," I said, stifling another yawn.

"Nah," he said. "It's stupid."

I sat up straight, pulling slightly away from him and angling my body so I could see his face. "Tell me."

"Okay, fine," he said. "Legend has it that if you kiss

someone atop the falls on Christmas Day you're destined to be together forever."

"What?" I said scrunching my nose. "You just made that up."

"No," he said, shaking his head and laughing. "It's a real thing. And why would I make that up? It's not like I'm telling you so we can kiss—and then I'd be stuck with you forever."

I reached up and lightly punched him in the arm. "You're mean, Broll."

He chuckled and then leaned in, planting a soft kiss on my forehead.

I pushed him away and then stood up and held out my hand.

"What are you doing?"

"Get up. You're gonna kiss me on the top of those falls," I said, putting on my most demanding tone and pointing up to where the falls started.

"Why? It's just a silly legend," he said as I grabbed his hands and helped pull him to standing.

"Because," I said. "Tonight has been magical—the community center has a fighting chance, Miss Anna Cate now has a fighting chance, and we are going to kiss on the top of the falls so we can have that same chance," I said this as I marched him over to the stairs.

We climbed the narrow staircase, me in front, him behind, holding hands as we went up.

When we got the top, I turned around and faced him.

"You sure you want to do this?" he asked, the corner of his mouth moving upward.

I nodded my head, "More sure than I've been about

anything in a long time." I didn't smile when I said this. My face was serious now. I meant it.

"Good," he said, and then he grabbed me and kissed me so perfectly, so tenderly, it didn't matter if the legend was true or not. I knew this was exactly where I was supposed to be.

I was home.

Valentine's Day

VALENTINE'S, SHMALENTINE'S. IT'S JUST ANOTHER day.

That was what I kept telling myself when I hadn't heard from Andy all day. All freaking day. Not a call, not a note, nada. I kept expecting flowers or chocolates or something to arrive at my door. But as of five-thirty that evening, there'd been nothing.

"Another sigh?" Miss Anna Cate said from the couch where she was sitting, reading a book, a blanket tucked around her. Her coloring looked good, so much better than it had been only a couple of months ago. A fully functioning kidney would be the reason for that. The surgery was a success.

"Sorry," I said, not even realizing I'd sighed. I plopped down in the armchair across from her. "It's just that, this is my first Valentine's with Andy."

"I thought you said you didn't care. That it was 'just a day'."

"It is . . . I don't. It's just . . ."

"It's just that you had expectations that aren't being met."

I huffed. "No. I mean, well . . . I guess. Even though I don't really care about this stupid holiday, I had some hope of . . . something."

"What did Piper say?"

I'd just gotten off the phone with Piper. She was getting all dressed up to go on a super hot date. One that her very wealthy boyfriend had all planned out. I was excited for her, but it also rubbed in the fact that I had no plans, and Andy was completely MIA.

"She said that Andy would come through. And something about him being smitten."

"She was always a smart one, that Piper of ours," Miss Anna Cate said, giving me a wink.

Piper was smart. But now that she had left her job at the resort where Andy worked and had moved to Nashville to work for her boyfriend's company, she no longer had real information for me and was only going by her gut.

Miss Anna Cate gave me a knowing smile. "Another sigh?"

"Sorry," I said. I stood up from the chair. "I guess I'll go unpack." At least I had that to keep me occupied.

Yes, there was much unpacking to do. I was officially back in Christmas Falls. All my boxes had been moved from San Francisco thanks to Andy and the longest road trip ever. So many hours in the car. It also didn't help that my mother had called nearly every hour of the drive to make sure we were okay. Once she knew we were, she'd launch into a lecture about my choices. But when we finally got into the Falls after marathon driving for three days, it was dusk and the streetlights were making the snow on the ground sparkle like it had been dusted with glitter—I was almost overwhelmed by how right it all felt.

A half hour later, I heard the doorbell ring and I jumped up from the floor where I was sorting through junk that I had haphazardly thrown in a box in my haste to pack everything quickly.

"Finally!" I yelled as I ran out of my room and toward the front door. I could hear Miss Anna Cate chuckling as I raced down the hall.

I was going to yell at him. But maybe kiss him first. And then yell at him for making me wait so long.

But when I opened the door, there was no one there.

"Andy?" I called out, sticking my upper body out the door and doing a quick search. There was no sign of anyone, not even sounds of footsteps crunching in the snow as they fled the area.

My shoulders slumped. Of all the times for some stupid high school kid to doorbell ditch us—

Something red caught my eye. I looked down and there on the step was a single red envelope that said *open me.*

I snatched it up and brought it in the house, shutting the door behind me.

"Whatcha got there?" Miss Anna Cate asked from her perch on the couch. Instead of a book, there was now a teacup in her hand.

"An envelope," I said, staring at it.

"I gathered that." Her voice oozed with sarcasm. "Ya gonna stare at it all day?"

I shook my head. "No, I guess I should open it." I looked down at the envelope as a thought suddenly occurred to me. "But what if it's for you?" I held the envelope out toward her.

"Honey, I haven't had a suitor in decades. I'm not anticipating any in the near future either. Open it," she said with a demanding nod.

I grabbed the envelope and ripped it open, pulling out a folded white piece of paper.

"What does it say?" Miss Anna Cate asked, now sounding a bit impatient.

I looked at the paper with just four simple lines, and read them aloud to the apparently grouchy old woman who was now my roommate.

A poet I am not
But since I like you a lot
Meet me at the place where
The chocolate is hot

P.S. Bring your coat.

"Oh," Miss Anna Cate said, slapping her leg with her free hand. "A treasure hunt."

"A treasure hunt?" I looked down at the note. A treasure hunt . . . I bit my bottom lip as I pictured Andy leaving this on the door and running away.

"Well, don't leave him waiting, dear. Get your coat."

I grabbed my coat and ran out the door yelling a quick goodbye to Miss Anna Cate as I did.

I had to give Andy credit; this was cute. But the clue was much too easy. Obviously, he was at Tinsel's Coffee Shop. I raced over as fast as my legs could carry me, huffing in the cold, damp air.

I opened the door to the coffee shop, a smile on my face as the familiar sound of bells jingled. It smelled like coffee and sweetness, and the warm air wrapped around me like a blanket. I could just picture him sitting there, waiting for me. Two cups of hot chocolate on the table in front of him.

But when I looked around, there wasn't any sign of him. No one with warm hazel eyes and dark brown hair sat anywhere in the vicinity.

"London?" A young teenage girl with curly auburn hair asked from behind the counter.

"Yeah?" I said, walking over to her.

"This is for you," she said, handing me another red envelope that said *open me* on the front.

I took it from her and opened it up, taking about as little care as I did with the first one. This note also had four lines.

It's cold outside
But it's extra warm where I am
Meet me at the place
The sugar cookies are baked . . . in

P.S. I told you I wasn't a poet.

I giggled to myself as I headed out of Tinsel's and ran down the street toward the grocery store where the bakery was. When I got there, once again there was no Andy to be found, but a red-cheeked Mrs. Mitchem had another envelope for me.

This envelope, with as equally terrible of a rhyme as the last, sent me to the diner where Clara gave me another note that took me to Poinsettia Cottage. There I found another envelope hanging on the door, which sent me to the community center.

I imagined the community center, all lit up with twinkling lights, a table for two in the middle. Soft music coming from the sound system. This had to be the final place. The perfect place, really. I'd finally get to see Andy. And I was going to kiss his face off once I found him. All the work he had to do to plan all this . . . This was, by far, the best Valentine's Day ever.

But when I got to the community center, it was completely dark. Taped to the door was another envelope. This one said:

> *You've done well in your quest*
> *Your journey is nearing the end*
> *Come find me in the place*
> *Where our first kiss happened.*

> *P.S. I'll be the one in the coat. With the glasses.*

The Falls. Of course! Of course that's where this would end. How did I even think the community center was the perfect spot?

I ran up the pathway and slowed as I came around the corner, my heart picking up its pace. This time he'd be there.

And there he was. The half-frozen falls, tall and grand, were twinkling behind him, the lone lamp lighting up his face enough that I could see that broad smile of his that I adored so much.

My heart did a sputtering jumping thing and an odd sensation washed over me. One I wasn't quite sure I'd ever felt before.

Love. I loved him.

I freaking loved Andy Broll.

I think I'd been feeling this way for a while, but I hadn't recognized it because I'd never been in love with anyone else. Not like this, at least. And I was going to tell him right now. I wasn't going to be one of those girls who kept it in and waited until he told me. I needed him to know now and the words were just waiting to burst out of me.

I walked up to him, put my arms around his neck, and planted a kiss on his lips that was only meant to be a quick kiss, but basically morphed into something quite a bit more than that as his gloved hands moved up my back. His lips felt like oxygen, which was the cheesiest thought I'd ever had. But it was true. It felt like they gave me air, like they gave me life.

When we pulled away, our rapid breaths intertwining in the cold air, I looked up at him. "Andy, I—"

"I love you, London," he said before I could get the words out.

"What?" I asked, taking a step back.

"I'm in love with you," Andy said, the most serious expression I'd ever seen on his face. He wrapped his hands around my arms, not allowing me to take another step back.

I let my shoulders fall and scrunched my face. How had he . . .

"You . . . you don't have to love me back," he said, the words rushing out of his mouth, a look of panic suddenly on his face. "I mean, if this is too soon, if you feel like—"

My eyes went wide. "No," I said, grabbing him around the waist. "No, I love you too. I was . . . well, you cut me off."

"What?"

"When I saw you standing there at the falls after all this," I gestured around me, referring to all the plans he had put into place to get me here, "I just knew. I think I've known for a while."

"You love me?" He looked like he was trying to reconcile what I'd said, like he almost didn't believe me.

I nodded.

"So why the weird reaction?" He cocked his head to the side and I could see his eyes squinting through those square-rimmed glasses of his.

I pushed out my lips in a pseudo-pout. "I was gonna say it first."

Andy's mouth pulled up into a broad smile—one that reached his eyes—and I couldn't help but echo with my own grin.

"Well, I'm really sorry about that," he said, not looking sorry at all.

He leaned down and placed a soft kiss on my lips.

175

"Say it again," he said in a quiet voice, his lips hovering millimeters from mine.

"I love you," I whispered.

"I love you, too."

We smiled at each other like a couple of lovesick teenagers. This really was the best Valentine's Day ever. At least, so far. I hoped there would be many more memorable ones to come.

Andy let out a breath. "Did you like it?"

"The treasure hunt?"

"Yeah," he said, his arms going tighter around me.

"I liked it very much," I said. "But this part, right now with you . . . this is the best part." I leaned my forehead against his. "I love you," I said again, wanting to say it over and over and maybe climb up to the top of the falls and scream it out over all of Christmas Falls.

"Me too," he said pulling his forehead away and looking into my eyes. "But . . ."

"But what?" I asked, feeling confused. Why would there be a *but*?

"But when we look back on this day, I think what we both will remember most is that—"

"Is what?" I said, cutting him off. What was he getting at?

"Is that . . . I said it first," he said with a wink.

And then before I could even protest, he grabbed me and kissed me soundly.

ABOUT THE AUTHOR

Becky Monson is a mother of three and a wife to one but would ditch them all for Henry Cavill. She used to write at night but now she's too dang tired, so she fits in writing between driving kids around to activities and running a household. With a talent for procrastination, Becky finds if she doesn't watch herself, she can waste an entire afternoon binge-watching Netflix. She's a USA Today bestseller and an award-winning author, and when she does actually get off Netflix to write, she uses humor and true life experiences to bring her characters to life.

Becky wishes she had a British accent and a magic spell to do her laundry. She has been trying to give up Diet Coke for the past ten years but has failed miserably.

www.beckymonson.com

Want to read another story set in the town of
Christmas Falls?
Check out *Holiday Honeymoon for One.*
Available on Amazon.

Made in the USA
Middletown, DE
18 March 2023

27051400R00106